D0990536

# QUICK BROWN FOX

*Recent Titles by Susan Kelly*

HOPE AGAINST HOPE

TIME OF HOPE

HOPE WILL ANSWER

KID'S STUFF

DEATH IS SWEET

THE GHOSTS OF ALBI *

* *available from Severn House*

# QUICK BROWN FOX

Susan Kelly

This first world edition published in Great Britain 1999 by
SEVERN HOUSE PUBLISHERS LTD of
9–15 High Street, Sutton, Surrey SM1 1DF.
First published in the USA 1999 by
SEVERN HOUSE PUBLISHERS INC., of
595 Madison Avenue, New York, NY 10022.



British Library Cataloguing in Publication Data

Kelly, Susan, 1955-
Quick brown fox
1. Detective and mystery stories
1. Title
823.9'14 [F]

ISBN 0-7278-5404-6



Typeset by Palimpsest Book Production Ltd
Polmont, Stirlingshire, Scotland.
Printed and bound in Great Britain by
MPG Books Ltd, Bodmin, Cornwall.

# Foreword

Two men sit in the bar of a golf club sipping Scotch and water. One is sixty, thick around the middle but strong looking. His florid face, framed in white hair, is largely innocent of wrinkles. He wears a red and yellow sweater in a diamond pattern, the caricature of a golfer in a situation comedy.

The other is a good ten years younger, of medium height and build, his short dark hair only flecked with grey. He pulls at his long nose when he's thinking. His exceptional good looks are lasting into middle age. His pullover is a tasteful solid, teal-blue lambswool, his blue and white check shirt visible at the neck and cuffs.

You might think he looks familiar, that you surely know his face from somewhere.

They're in good humour after their regular eighteen holes and are talking easily and comfortably about nothing. The older man offers a cigarette from a silver case but is waved away. He laughs. Given up? He's heard that one before.

He twists in his seat and eyes the dining room, suggesting lunch, but his companion, having glanced at his watch, excuses himself, drains his glass and leaves with a last friendly wave and promises of renewed competition at the weekend.

He collects a tan suede jacket from the cloakroom where the attendant gives him her special smile and raises a hand to fuss her shoulder-length blond hair.

He gets into his blue Ford Sierra and drives the few miles home, his radio tuned to Classic FM. He hums along with the music as the Suffolk landscape unfolds around him. It's almost Christmas but the weather is mild if a little damp and the autumn colours linger on the trees. He won this morning by two holes and feels pleased with himself and the world.

The golf club is less than three miles from his home but a wide river – the Deben, not the Styx – separates the two and he must drive north for some minutes to bridge it before heading south again on what he likes to call the *rive gauche*. He's hungry and hopes his wife will have his lunch ready.

But although her car's in the drive, his homecoming call elicits no response and his old spaniel bitch doesn't come waddling to greet him and be made a fuss of. He concludes that they're out walking.

The whitewashed cottage is cool, as if she's been out for some time, and he turns up the thermostat, hearing the boiler shudder reluctantly into action. He goes into the kitchen and finds no sign of lunch in preparation.

He's not worried by this as his wife has been showing signs of housework fatigue lately and probably wishes to demonstrate her independence. She's no doubt having lunch with her best friend. He'll show her that he's perfectly capable of fending for himself.

Which is just as well.

He forages in the fridge and finds cheese and tomatoes. There's fresh crusty bread in the bin and home-made chutney in the store cupboard. He will feast.

Afterwards, he puts the kettle on for coffee. As he fills it at the tap he happens to glance out of the window. A mature apple tree stands to one side of the back garden, under it a brace of graves, the last resting place of much-loved canine companions. There is also a green rubbish sack slumped in a half-full heap against the trunk. Clearly his wife has been having a blitz on fallen leaves, but why not simply pile them on the bonfire?

He decides that he'll go and investigate when he's finished his coffee.

Then there's a shrill, staccato ringing at the doorbell.

And the nightmare begins.

# Down to earth

For two and a half days he has been a god; it will take me a month to humanise him. For a long weekend in a hotel on the outskirts of Miami they have worshipped him: women of all shapes, ages and types. Now he's come home to his wife, to his whitewashed cottage in Suffolk, tired, complaining about the length of the flight, its discomfort and poor food.

He thinks he should travel first class. He thinks that the handmaidens of the airline aren't as young and pretty as they used to be, aren't as servile or as svelte. Something to do with Political Correctness.

In a bad mood at having to come down from Olympus.

"God, I'm bushed! That really is the last time, Jenny." He says that and always he goes back. Who wouldn't want to be deified, once a year?

I run him a bath and pour him a whisky and soda. While he bathes and drinks I sit on the lavatory seat and he tells me about it: how the shower in his room didn't work and there was no Scotch in the minibar, only grainy Bourbon; how the meat at the banquet was unidentifiable, like the time we went to Russia. Gradually he begins to laugh at his misfortunes, recovering his customary good temper.

He's Andrew (Don) Donleavy, a jobbing actor, one of those thousands who set out from drama school full of expectation but don't quite make it, are never in exactly the right place at the right time because, make no mistake, you need luck. Adverts pay the mortgage or, more often these days, voice-overs. Because although his face is lined now and sagging a little, his beautiful voice grows richer and deeper with the years.

He asks too casually, "Did my agent ring?"

"Um, no." The usual answer.

"Oh."

"Were you expecting her to?"

"Oh, no. Not specially." He drains his glass and holds it out. "I wouldn't say no to a refill."

As I go obediently downstairs, he begins to rub herbal shampoo into his thick hair.

When I say he never made it, it's with one caveat. In the early eighties he appeared in a Thames TV series called *Space Pirates* which was axed after two seasons and never repeated. The critics jeered but the public loved it, and five years later – when it was too late to revive it and bring in more work and money – it had gained a cult following on both sides of the Atlantic.

Don played the leader of this band of cutthroats, who roared round the galaxy in a clapped-out spacecraft, looting, pillaging, murdering and kidnapping. He was thirty-five then, dark-haired, handsome and sleek. He wore a doublet and hose with sexy boots that emphasised his shapely legs, not unlike the sort of thing he wore when he was Second Spear Carrier at the RSC soon after we were married.

Now he's forty-eight and has gained a stone and a half, mostly round the middle, acquired a lot of grey hairs around the edges and, as I said before, more than a few wrinkles. But those make no difference to the fans. To them he is, and always will be, the dashing young Captain Will Davenant, his lip curling cruelly as he makes some subordinate walk the plank (that is to say be marooned on a hostile planet peopled with carnivorous plants).

The special effects were, to put it tactfully, homely – more Gerry Anderson than Industrial Light and Magic. When the show came out on video in 1990 we got the full set so that Don could admire himself in his prime, and I amuse myself on lonely days playing them frame by frame to see the joins.

That was the high spot of his career and he's not done much TV work since, but the fans never forget. Every year he's asked to be guest of honour at a convention, along with the stars of *Dr Who*, *Blake's Seven*, *Red Dwarf* and a few too obscure even to mention. He goes – "work commitments permitting", which means almost always.

He sips at his refreshed glass, his wet hair sticking up in unruly tufts. His face is glowing from the steam of the hot bath. I want to reach out and touch his big pink body.

"What a hothouse those bloody conventions are!" he says.

"What was it like?"

"The usual. Mayhem. A few loony tunes. An awful lot of autographs." Anything up to two thousand devotees buying books, badges, plastic models of the *Bounty*, begging for signatures, staring at him as he eats his dinner.

He laughs. "One Australian girl had me write my name way up on her thigh in black felt-tip!"

"I hope she's going to wash eventually."

"And it was only after I'd reluctantly agreed that I realised she wasn't wearing any knickers. I kept my hand steady and my eyes averted."

"If you'd said, 'All right, love, how about it?' she'd probably have run a mile."

"Prob'ly, but I wasn't about to take that risk."

He leans back and closes his eyes. I examine his face for signs of guilt, but what might those signs be? Oh, for the art to find the mind's construction in the face. Quoting from the Scottish Play: that'll bring no good.

They like to touch him, as if he was an idol, able to cure their ills; even the hem of his garment.

No one thinks what it's like to be the wife of a god, or if they do they think it's a good job to have, with excellent hours and conditions, terrific perks. They don't think what it must be like always to play a supporting role, thought of only in relation to him, as if I had no identity of my own. As if I cease to exist when he is not here to look at me.

The fans use these conventions to raise money for charity which makes it all the harder to say no. Besides, who's going to turn down a weekend of worship?

I know I wouldn't.

# Supporting part

I was an actor myself when I met Don, more than twenty-five years ago. I'd like to say I gave up my career to support his but it wouldn't be true. I couldn't be bothered with the hard and boring bits: that's the truth.

I could have coped with being a glamorous film star with my own trailer and a driver and people saying, "Yes, Miss Farrell . . . at once, Miss Farrell. Steven Spielberg on the line for you, Miss Farrell; shall I tell him to call back?' But paying your dues in rep – rotten parts, rotten boarding houses, drunken passes from rotten old lechers – defeated me and I gave it up.

We didn't have children. I wonder what those fans would think if they knew that dashing Captain Will Davenant fires blanks from his Freudian laser pistol.

I used to go with him in the early days, to the conventions. I thought it might be fun, but they hated me. I mean it. They *loathed* me with a burning envy that seared through my thin skin. I was surrounded by hundreds of women who wanted me dead. They would stare at me covertly, contemptuously, wondering what a man like him was doing with me: a woman past forty, a little overweight, a bit greying.

Just like him.

I could see their thoughts, like cartoon balloons above their heads. *He's been married to her for twenty years so he can't possibly love her any more, not in any* real *sense, not* sexually. *They probably don't even sleep together.*

When you're young it doesn't occur to you that middle-aged people can love each other too, that they want to *make* love, perhaps not as often as you do, but with considerably more skill and pleasure. I was the same at their age: unable to imagine my parents in such silly postures.

Some of them were as young as seventeen; most of them were pretty. They would stand talking to him, tongue-tied at first until he put them at their ease with his quick charm, their clean bodies closer than would be normal in social situations, turned towards his, mirroring his actions, saying, "I want you, this is my room number, I'm available."

Is he unfaithful to me? I've never asked him: if he said yes, I don't think I could bear it; if he said no, I don't think I could believe him.

Is he careful in this disease-ridden age?

Even the gays want him. There used to be a rumour – perhaps there still is – that he's secretly one of their fraternity, that I'm what we call in our trade a *beard* – someone used as a smokescreen for an actor's true sexuality.

That neatly explains the childlessness, you see.

They cannot bear to think that they can't have him, any of them, that he belongs to me.

So I don't go with him any more; there's so much to do in the garden.

We had to go ex-directory when *Pirates* really took off. By halfway through the first season the phone was ringing all day with girls wanting to hear his voice. I gave up answering it in the end; if he wasn't there I let it ring rather than face the coldness of their disappointment, the heat of their hostility.

They think they own him. They want to know everything about him: not only his career, his life as an actor, but the most personal things, as the edges of fantasy and reality blur. It has its upside. How many actors outside the Hollywood A-list can boast their own fan club?

So Don is home from the convention and I'm glad to see him as I pick up a flannel and begin to soap his back. I love him. I've never loved anyone else. I never had a 'proper' boyfriend before him. I gave him my virginity in the summer of 1970.

He knows I'll put up with anything.

# Resting

He's got nothing lined up in the foreseeable future. He's resting. That doesn't mean that he will help in the garden.

Our village – Stratford St James – is ten miles north-east of Ipswich off the road to Bawdsey, near the market town of Woodbridge. We've lived here for fifteen years, which qualifies us as old-established residents since the place is picturesque and therefore popular with commuters, incomers. It's not one of those Gothic places of legend where everyone marries their cousin and you're not accepted by the locals until you've lived there for four generations.

Since it has no particular features to attract tourists, and much competition from better-known villages, it is little visited and quiet.

Our house – The White House – is half a mile out of the village, set back from the B-road, down a lane marked Stratford End, which peters out in farmland a couple of hundred yards beyond our gate. It's late Victorian, put up by a builder called Joshua Knotter in the 1880s, for reasons that aren't easy to discern. The date and his initials are carved on the lintel above the front door.

Why did he build ten minutes' walk from the village green when there must have been land to spare in those days before planning regulations? Why did he build only one house when there is space for a dozen? Was he one of nature's loners, designing a hideaway for himself, safe behind a white picket fence and a lot of noisy Southwold gravel? If so, the parish records suggest that he never moved in.

A mystery that will remain for ever unsolved.

The house isn't large either, despite the generous building plot: downstairs there's a decent-sized kitchen where I spend most of my time when I'm indoors, a sitting/dining room with French doors out onto a paved area, and a minuscule study for Don. Upstairs are three bedrooms, of which the third is more like a cupboard, and one typically Victorian bathroom – not intended for loiterers.

The large garden was one of the attractions.

It was all we could afford when we moved out of London and, since there were to be no children wanting space, we never found the need or the energy to move.

We *almost* did when my father died and we thought we should find a place with a granny flat so we could offer my mother a home with us; but we'd barely put it on the market when she too died, in her sleep one night, as if her heart could no longer see the point in beating, and plans for upheaval could be shelved.

"So what's new with you?" he asks at last.

"Nothing much." I hold up a warm towel for him to step into. "The day anything interesting happens round here . . ."

I don't want it to. It's like that Chinese curse you put on your worst enemy: May you live in interesting times.

The village is a disparate lot of houses grouped round a green with a pond. There's the pub – The Old Piper – and a village store cum sub-post-office. There is also one of those huge churches in which East Anglia abounds, big enough to seat the villagers twenty times over, as if they were expecting a population explosion of nuclear proportions. There's a service there once a month since we don't have a full-time vicar and the Old Rectory has belonged, for more than twenty years, to Mr Herzog.

I've been known to go to morning service myself if I'm up in time, although I wasn't raised in the Church of England. We're ecumenical now.

"And my girls? They've been okay?" I say they have and he asks with mock sternness, "Are we making progress with our obedience training?" We have two golden spaniels, both female. Aggie is an old lady of ten, while Scamper's a baby of three months. She's the one who's not getting the hang of coming to heel yet.

Aggie's sister Martha died of cancer in the spring. As always in such a situation, I swore I would never have another dog to break my heart; then Don came home three weeks ago with a tiny ginger scrap under his coat, just weaned from her mother, frightened and missing her family.

"No," I said as soon as I saw her, and again, "no."

"She's the runt of the litter. The breeder was going to have her put down. I had to exercise all my charm to rescue her and I had to promise to have her spayed as soon as she reaches puberty, not to breed from her. Here."

He dropped the puppy in my lap where it fell on its back, showing a lot of white underbelly. Its legs began to whirl in different directions as it tried to right itself. I helped it up. It licked my palm. Its fur was as soft as the finest mink.

"Of course," he said in a carefully bored tone, "I can take it back."

"And let her kill her? Over my dead body."

He grinned and produced a tin of special puppy food and that was that. Scamper was part of the family.

We've always had bitches. I suppose he likes to surround himself with adoring females and, boy, do those dogs adore him.

No, we don't think of them as substitute children, although dogs only die, they don't grow up and leave home.

He asks, "Any post for me?"

"The usual. Nothing that needs your lordship's personal attention."

I answer the simple fan letters and he signs them. Sometimes he reads them but mostly he doesn't bother. The ones that are pure filth go straight on the fire.

# The newcomer

I usually do a big shop once a week in Ipswich but I feel an obligation to put some business the way of the village store, so I always "forget" at least one thing; and then there are stamps which cost the same everywhere, and newspapers. The village store is the place to collect the local gossip, which is the main thing.

So I set off for the village one morning in late June, a week after the convention, leaving Don in bed having a bit of a lie-in. He might, he said, put on an ugly sweater and wander over to the golf club later.

The only shopping he would consider doing is a trip to the wine merchants. He knows a bit about wine, having done an evening class. He doesn't know about the wines of Burgundy, since he missed those two weeks owing to a booking at the Liverpool Everyman – a bizarre new comedy/thriller which succeeded in being neither and never did achieve its promised transfer to Shaftesbury Avenue.

If it had, he'd have missed the rest of the term and we would be able to drink nothing but claret.

I walked the half-mile to the village green along the pavementless road, edged with low hedges. I kept to the right, facing oncoming traffic, like the native-born countrywoman that I am, but no cars passed me that day.

Fifteen years ago the fields on either side were full of wheat; now they're EC set-aside – the farmer paid by Brussels to grow nothing – and have run into a wilderness that welcomes butterflies and birds and rare flowers, with mice and voles happily nesting in the old drainage ditches.

I took the dogs along for company and to have their morning ablutions in the hedgerow. I kept Scamper on her lead but Aggie trotted free at my heel, long schooled in road sense. I tied them to the post outside the shop and went in to buy some ham for lunch.

I walked into the middle of an animated conversation between Mrs Price the shopkeeper, Mr Herzog, a retired stockbroker and old bachelor, and Leonora Apter, a sensible woman in her early thirties, who is something to do with the Aldeburgh festival on the organisational rather than the artistic side.

Leo lives with her elderly parents in the "big" house – Stratford House – and she and I are sort of friends, being more in tune with each other's personalities than other candidates for friendship that the village affords. Sometimes we go riding together. Colonel Apter is the owner of those non-productive but lucrative fields.

"Mrs Donleavy," Mrs Price said as soon as I reached

the counter, "have you heard that Madder Cottage is sold?"

"Good," I said, since the place was starting to become an eyesore.

Don remarked once that no one could be madder than Miss Aspinall, the former owner of the cottage. She'd been an insanitary old woman, rumoured to be well past ninety, whose stray cats were too numerous to count. She didn't socialise with the rest of the village. I once attempted to speak to her soon after we came to live here but she shook her stick at me and shouted something incomprehensible.

Do people go mad because they're lonely, or are they left lonely because they're mad?

Rumour had it that she'd been born in Madder Cottage and, most certainly, she died there, although it was some two weeks before anyone raised the alarm, broke in and found her body. I say *some* two weeks since it was an exceptionally warm summer and, given the condition of the body, the pathologist wasn't prepared to venture a nearer date of death.

People think that in a small village like this everybody knows your business, but they don't, not unless you tell them.

That had been more than a year earlier. A number of Aspinall nephews and nieces had had the house up for sale ever since, but they were greedy and the market was sluggish and I don't think anyone could face the squalor. On the other hand the place had a lot of potential for someone with the necessary time, money and strong stomach to do it up, preferably someone who wasn't afraid of ghosts.

It dated from the late seventeenth century and browsed its way through a series of dark rooms in an easy and picturesque manner. It fronted the green, with a fine view across to the church and the pub, while the garden sloped down to the stream – the Madder – that fed the village pond.

Despite their comparative names, Madder Cottage was twice the size of The White House. I'd looked at it once or twice, in passing, and felt tempted by its powerful atmosphere, by the characteristic tall chimneys and the steep-pitched roof which had once been thatched but was now haphazardly pantiled.

What attracted me above all was the original pargeting – the raised plasterwork decoration – which consisted of odd geometric shapes between the small windows. They'd been left to rot and needed to be restored and picked out in black against the white brickwork to give them their full glory once more.

"The new owner's an artist by all accounts," Mrs Price was saying, her blatant freckles throbbing with excitement. Her little eyes were bright, preparing to introduce a fabulous new character into her personal soap opera.

Good, I thought. He'll make a proper job of restoring the place.

"She'll be wanting a studio, then," Mr Herzog said,

inadvertently correcting my mistake as to the gender of the new owner. "Perhaps one of the outbuildings."

"I hope she's a proper artist and not one of these people as throws paint at the canvas any old how," Mrs Price said, interrupting. "Running bicycle wheels over it and I don't know what."

Leo, Mr Herzog and I looked sympathetically at each other and murmured something that Mrs Price chose to take as agreement. Not that I knew anything about modern art, any more than, I suppose, did my co-conspirators, but we knew that it would be philistine to say so.

"When's she moving in?" Leo asked. "Surely she'll need to get the builders in first."

"Oh, right away," the shopkeeper contradicted her. "She's sold her place in London and she says she don't mind camping out for a bit, roughing it. I hope she's got plenty of cash in her pocket, that's all I can say, 'cause she's gonna need it."

It had been thought for a while that Madder Cottage might have to be demolished but, whoever the seventeenth-century jobbing builder who put it up had been, he, and his house, had been made of sterner stuff.

"She's got the gardeners in already," Mrs Price added. "That strange Aysgarth boy, and he won't be cheap."

"The garden is the most frightful mess," Mr Herzog pointed out. "I doubt Miss Aspinall pulled a weed in the last twenty years. I once offered to help but – well, you know what she was like."

"Is she on her own?" I asked.

Mrs Price considered this. "Looks like that," she said at last.

"Is she a *young* lady?" Mr Herzog demanded.

Mrs Price pursed her lips and we realised that she hadn't met the woman in question and that this information wasn't straight from the horse's mouth.

"What's her name?" asked Leo, who was the one among us most likely to have heard of an artist.

"Suza Darc is what she calls herself. Can't say as I've ever heard of her." The name sounded vaguely familiar to me. "Odd sort of a name if you ask me," Mrs Price went on. "Perhaps it's a whatdyacallit? A *nomm de ploom*, stage name, sort of thing."

Leo Apter clicked her tongue in exasperation. "Oh, Mrs Price, Suza Darc isn't an *artist*; she's a writer, a novelist."

"Well, I've still never heard of her," Mrs Price said.

"She's well known, among those of us who can read," Leo said tartly. "Do you know her work, Jenny?"

"It rings a vague bell." I remembered now that I'd started one of her novels after it had been shortlisted for some prize or other the previous year, but I'd given up after three chapters. It had unsettled me in some ill-defined way, made me uncomfortable. I'd put it straight in the jumble box and folded two holey jerseys of Don's over it so that it couldn't get out again.

In a village this size it's impossible to avoid people. Friends who've stuck with living in London can't understand that: they don't talk to the people next door unless they feel like it; but in deepest Suffolk you have to be civil to people you would cross the street to avoid elsewhere.

I hoped Suza Darc was nothing like her books.

# Whisky eyes

I found out fast enough since Don brought her in for morning coffee the following week, which wasn't like him; he doesn't go out of his way to do small kindnesses.

He'd gone down to the village to buy some cigarettes, having deliberately let himself run out on the grounds that he was giving up smoking. Then some minor setback – a part he'd been keen on but had auditioned badly for – sent him reaching for a fag and there were none there.

Since I'd studiously avoided volunteering to go and fetch them for him, he'd been reduced to going himself – a bit like the Queen popping out for half a pound of sprouts.

He was gone longer than I expected since he makes a point of not standing gossiping in the village shop for ages, even if he has to be downright rude to get away. Mrs Price makes allowances for his rudeness since he's almost famous and thespians are permitted their eccentricities, especially men.

Finally, I heard the creak of the wooden gate, a

scrunching of gravel and I had the kettle on by the time the kitchen door opened.

"Get caught by the village Mafia?" I asked. "Oh, sorry! I didn't realise—"

"This is Suza Darc," Don said, "Our new neighbour. I've brought her home for coffee since the electricity isn't turned on in her house. It seems she's bought old Miss Aspinall's cottage."

I'd told him of the conversation in the shop but he'd clearly not been listening and thought that this woman was his own invention.

"This is my wife, Jenny," he concluded.

We shook hands. She looked much more relaxed than I felt, and as though she might not be afraid of anything. She was a tall woman of about forty, and large without being in the least fat. Black hair sprinkled with white – a sable silver'd, as Horatio says – hung loose and heavy about her shoulders, framing an unmade-up face with good smooth skin. Eyes that were brown and flecked with gold – the colour of whisky – looked directly at me, returning my scrutiny. They were not unfriendly.

A handsome woman, I thought, if formidable.

"I hope it's not inconvenient—" she began in a deep voice that seemed to start well down in her chest as if she'd studied acting or singing at some time.

"Of course it isn't," Don broke in. "I wouldn't have asked you if it was." Which was perfectly true since he never does anything unless it suits him.

"The electricity was supposed to have been switched back on yesterday at the latest," she went on, "but nothing's happened and they can't do it now until later this afternoon, it seems. Or possibly tomorrow."

"*Won't*, not *can't*," Don said.

"The place will have to be rewired, anyway," she said. "I'm afraid it's a death trap the way it is."

"Of course it's not inconvenient," I echoed. "I'm so pleased to meet you. Won't you sit down?" I cleared a pile of ironing off a chair and she sat. Aggie immediately came and rubbed against her legs. She leant down to pet her with long, firm strokes. I saw that her hands were strong and brown, the nails clipped short. I don't suppose you can type with long nails.

"What's your name, pretty girl?" Suza Darc asked.

Aggie, despite her advanced years, rolled on her back in ecstasy.

"She likes you," I said with a nervous laugh. "She's a bit shy normally. Her name's Aggie. There's another one about somewhere – much more extrovert, as a rule."

"I get on with dogs for some reason," Suza Darc said. "I had a couple of hounds follow me six miles across Dartmoor once, couldn't get them to leave off and go back, whatever I did. They scuttled over cattle grids and limboed under gates. I had to drive them home in the end. Then they didn't want to get out of the car. Oh, and one of them peed in the back seat!"

"The offspring of the Hound of the Baskervilles?" Don said, also sitting down at the table, and they both laughed, not because it was particularly funny but to signal goodwill.

She had a rich and unashamed laugh.

"But there wasn't a Hound of the Baskervilles," I said, though apparently unheard. "It was a trick."

"Trouble is," she said, pulling a Liberty silk handkerchief out of her pocket, "I'm asthmatic and anything furry can set it off at close quarters." I called the reluctant Aggie away and she curled sulkily into her basket. Suza said, "I shall have to have Madder Cottage fumigated; it seems the previous owner was something of a cat lover."

"Bit of an understatement!" Don said. "She was the village witch and they were her familiars – all ninety-six of them."

"I wonder what happened to the cats after her death," I said, as I hadn't thought of this before.

"They faded away into the fifth dimension," my husband said indifferently, "like all supernatural creatures."

I suppose they strayed when the supply of food dried up, or starved. I'm not a cat person: cats seem to me to behave like depressed people, eating and sleeping all the time; while with a dog, all it needs is food, exercise, a stick to carry about and a human to worship and it's happy the livelong day.

Suza stretched out her long legs, seemingly comfortable in our company. They wore that dark blue shade of denim which is called indigo. She had on a sweatshirt in a paler blue and a cream sleeveless quilted jacket with a blue and cream scarf knotted at her neck. Her boots looked serious.

"I like to walk," she explained, following my eyes. "Miles 'n' miles 'n' miles. Helps me think. It's one of the reasons I moved out of London. I don't like hills, though. That's one of the reasons I settled on Suffolk. Very flat, Suffolk."

"What were the other reasons?" I asked, expecting family connections.

"I heard that it was *weird*."

The kettle boiled at that moment, saving me from having to answer this. I poured water into the cafetière. I took home-made biscuits out of the tin and put them on a plate while I waited for the coffee to brew. I took the best china from the Welsh dresser and hastily rinsed it under the cold tap. It was like the first time I met my prospective mother-in-law – also formidable – and I was terrified of doing or saying the wrong thing.

Don was detailing – badly, since he seldom uses them – the more popular local footpaths and offering to lend her maps.

"Andy tells me you're both actors," she said to me, taking her coffee with a smile of thanks. She picked up a biscuit and bit into it with strong teeth. Somehow I knew she wasn't the sort of woman who refused good food because she was watching her weight.

I realised that she was looking at me expectantly, that I had been asked a question. I racked my brains for what it was. "Oh, I haven't done anything for years," I said quickly. "I keep up my Equity card but I hardly know why."

"I used to be a *jeune premier*," Don said, "but I'm too long in the tooth now." This was said in his pitiful voice – the one that's supposed to make women exclaim, "Of course you aren't," and drag him off to bed to prove to him how virile he still is.

Suza Darc merely smiled gently and replied, "No one's going to ask you to be MacCauley Culkin's stunt double, Andy."

"I used to do my own stunts—" Don flexed his left arm "—until I managed to break my elbow one day."

"That taught him a lesson," I said.

"Most acting doesn't involve stunts, surely," she said.

"Oh, I'm talking about when I was Captain Will Davenant," he said.

She raised her eyebrows. I smiled to myself. Suza Darc hadn't heard of *Space Pirates*.

"And you," I broke in, changing the subject, "are a writer."

"For my sins."

Which seemed an odd thing for her to say since writers, like actors, seem to get paid large sums of money for doing the thing they love best in the world. Don and his friends try to make out what hard work it is, but all I can say is they should try doing some *real* hard work – a ten-hour shift on an assembly line, a day down a mine, a week spent washing up in a greasy spoon café.

"I must read some of your books," Don said, looking at her intently across the table. "What are their titles?" She reeled off about six names, unfamiliar except for the one I had hastily given to Oxfam. "Would they make good films?" Don asked, meaning: are there any good parts in them for me?

"Probably not. One was filmed a couple of years back but it wasn't a great success and went straight to video."

Not enough action; not enough plot.

She said, "You must let me give you some of my author's copies," as I imagine Don had intended. I made a protest which was more than token but she added, "I have more of them than I know what to do with. You can have a copy translated into Japanese if you like, or Danish. You'll be doing me a favour."

So that was settled.

"I saw she was moving in," he explained when she'd gone, "because the removal van was just pulling away, and I thought I'd be neighbourly. You know what it's like on moving day: you can't find a thing."

He must be bored, I thought, with resting. He was still sitting at the table and I ran my hand through his hair. He wore it short these days, bristly, but there was, as yet, no sign of a bald patch, for which I was thankful, never having fancied bald men.

He broke off his story. "Shit!" He slapped his fist to his brow in a theatrical gesture (King Lear beginning to wise up?). "I forgot my cigarettes after all that! Oh, well, perhaps I really will pack them in."

"Yeah, sure." I bent and kissed the top of his head. I put my hand under his jaw and pulled his dear face up to mine. I kissed his cleft chin, his nose that was a trifle too long to be perfect. I kissed his firm mouth with its full lips.

Then I let him go. He looked at me with bemusement for a moment then went on with his story. "I tried the doorbell but it wasn't working. The door wasn't locked and I pushed it open. She didn't hear me because she'd got a transistor radio tuned to Radio Three and was vigorously conducting part of Verdi's *Otello* with a fish slice in the middle of the biggest collection of tea chests I've ever seen, mostly full of books by the look of them."

I giggled. "I think I'd have slunk away."

"I thought about it," he admitted, "but I coughed instead. She wasn't the least bit embarrassed. In fact she waited until the end of the aria before she put the fish slice down and turned the sound off."

"She wasn't frightened to be crept up on by some strange man?"

"I get the impression she isn't afraid of anything," he said, curiously echoing my own thought.

"Is there any sign of a *Mr* Darc?"

"She's divorced."

I've always been wary of divorcees: they want everyone to be divorced so they won't be alone with their failure.

"Awfully nice woman," Don was saying. "Ought to shake this dreary village up a bit anyway."

"Sure, *Andy*."

"I told her everyone called me Don and she said in that case she'd be different."

"She's that all right," I said, since, like her novel, Suza Darc made me uneasy in a way I could not define.

# Friends

"You know, you made me nervous the first time we met."

Suza looked up from making bacon sandwiches – we alternated providing lunch and she wasn't much of a cook – and asked with a laugh, "Why?"

"I can't explain. You can be a bit intimidating, you know. Mrs Price is terrified of you."

"That nosy old bat! She doesn't like me because I won't tell her my life story and intimate secrets so she can spread them round the village. I gave her one of my early paperbacks and told her she'd find out everything there was to know about me from reading that. She's looked askance at me ever since." She tilted her head to one side, then the other, and squinted at me. "What does that mean, anyway? Why would you look at anyone *askance*?"

"Which book was it?" I asked, laughing.

"*The Four Friends*."

"The one where the woman murders her husband by choking him with a spider's web?"

"Is it possible, do you think—" Suza put on a look of comic dismay "—that Mrs Price took my words too literally?"

"You are awful, Suza."

"The next thing she said to me—" Suza mimicked Mrs Price's Suffolk accent rather well, along with her air of affronted dignity, making me wonder again if there was some long-but-not-lost acting training there "—was, 'It is *Mrs* Darc, is it? Widder, are you?' "

I curled my feet up under me on the small sofa she kept in the kitchen by the Aga and sipped my coffee. It was autumn now and set to be a cold one and I'd found a friend – a girlfriend I could giggle with and exchange confidences with – for the first time in years. If we weren't careful, we'd be fixing each other's hair.

I had been wary of women friends for so long, afraid that one of them would set her cap at Don. He liked to muscle in on any friendship I made, as if he feared to leave me alone with my confidantes, and I'm not sure that a man and a woman can be just friends, that some greater intimacy won't creep in.

"And who is she to talk?" Suza went on. "Where is *Mr* Price? That's what I'd like to know."

"He decamped . . . oh, about ten years ago."

"Another woman?"

"I don't think so." I giggled, remembering Sam Price with his honest round face and his red scalp, his chubby arms and Fair Isle tank tops, trying to imagine him with a mistress. "I don't think he needed an *excuse* to leave Mrs Price."

"Did anyone see him go, though? Did you see him pack up his traps and drive away?"

I tried to remember. It was a long time ago. "More of a moonlight flit, I think."

"There!" she said triumphantly. "She's got him buried in the back garden."

"You live in a fantasy world," I said affectionately.

I don't make friends easily although I have a large acquaintance in the neighbourhood and Don is gregarious and knows an awful lot of people in the business on cheek-kissing, mwah-mwah terms. I'm self-sufficient in an odd sort of way. I never mind doing things, going places, on my own. It wouldn't usually occur to me to offer friendship to a newcomer any more than the merest politeness demands.

I suppose there aren't many women in their forties in the village, or not ones who are at home all day, and Suza wasn't exactly spoilt for choice when it came to new friends. Whatever the reason it was she who sought me out and I suppose I was flattered, while remaining initially intimidated.

She asked me to suggest places she might visit, to get to know her new home. Of course I felt obliged to show her the obvious sights: Sutton Hoo, Ickworth, Lavenham, Melford, and what the tourist board calls Constable Country.

She was quiet at first, not foisting conversation on me,

nor asking too many questions of me, which is the one thing guaranteed to make me clam up. And soon I got used to her presence at my side, to her large comfortable body, with its loose easy walk, making me feel safe.

I began to show her my special places, the rivers, woods and shorelines of my adopted home, which was now hers too. And so it was that by the end of the summer we were firm friends.

Suza was like nobody I'd ever met: she was strong and honest, independent, totally without sentiment, believing that the truth should never shock. I'd read her books now and no longer knew what it was that had made me uneasy. Or, rather, I *did* know: it was that her characters were as brave, as sincere, as self-aware as she, and that takes a bit of getting used to.

She was there all the time too, available. She hardly ever went away, said she didn't like holidays, that she liked it *here*. If you need so desperately to get away from it all, she said, you should be making serious changes in your life, not loitering at the travel agents.

At first I was afraid to disturb her work, of being a latter-day person from Porlock, but she said she worked at night since she didn't need much sleep and that, anyway, three or four hours were all she could bear at one go.

"I don't believe anyone does more than four hours' productive work a day," she'd said, "however much time they may spend at the office. And what's the point of being self-employed if you chain yourself to a desk from nine to five, Monday to Friday?"

Don seemed to have lost interest in her and was inclined to complain that she was always at our house, which was one of the reasons, I suppose, that I felt she was not a threat. "The neighbours will think I'm running a *ménage à trois*," he grumbled.

"You should be so lucky!"

"Seriously, Jenny. Do you think she's the right sort of friend for you?"

"Now you sound like my father. I'm not fourteen any more. What are you – jealous?"

Madder Cottage had become habitable in a shorter time than I'd believed possible. It had been rewired and replumbed and a most efficient central heating system had been discreetly installed. The garden had been tamed, the pargeting remoulded and the decorating was progressing room by room.

People liked to do things for Suza. She quickly won their respect. *Her* builders didn't disappear halfway through a job to finish something else.

Her kitchen was now warm and welcoming – furnished, not with the inevitable fitted kitchen in rustic pine, but with free-standing units in limed oak, beautifully carved with flowers and leaves and trees. "You can take them with you when you move," I'd said approvingly, when first I saw them.

"I'm not going anywhere," she'd said with a laugh. "This is my last resting place. I've come here to die – though not for another forty years."

I asked her if Suza Darc was her real name and she

said not, mocking me. "It's *nobody's* real name, Jennifer; it doesn't even *sound* like a real name." But she wouldn't tell me what she was really called and though I spied casually on the letters that arrived for her, they were all in that name, as were the bills. "It's been my name since my first book was published twelve years ago," she said. "I'm not going to use my ex-husband's name, am I?"

Since there were no children she and her ex had no reason to keep in touch and she didn't even know where he was.

"What about your father's name?" I asked.

"He wasn't my real father," she said with a shrug, "only the man who was dumb enough to marry my mum when she got herself knocked up. I think that made him angry. To be fair, it would have made me angry. I left home on my eighteenth birthday. I left them a note saying, 'You have no power over me any more. You will never see me again. I'd like to kill you.'"

"Do you think you *could* kill someone?" I asked.

She didn't seem to find the question strange. "Only with my cooking!"

She seemed to have no family. In a way, I was glad since it meant I could be her family.

It occurred to me that for years I'd been lonely.

# Dangerous corner

Her husband had left her for another man. I suggested diffidently that she hadn't had much luck in life, but she brushed it off, obviously declining sympathy, and said, "I don't think about the bad bits. I forget them. The past can't hurt me."

She spread her arms wide to take in her small kingdom. "Look at me: I have enough money, work I enjoy, a home that'll be lovely one day, in about a million years' time, excellent health. If anything, I've been lucky. The last thing I want or need is a man in my life."

I wondered briefly if she was a lesbian but realised that it wasn't that which set her apart from other women. It was that she didn't defer to men, the way even the most sensible and liberated woman tends to do, didn't let them interrupt her, didn't go out of her way to make them feel important.

Which was probably why Don had decided he didn't much like her after all.

The fleeting idea that she might be a lesbian disturbed me and I realised that I had, in a sense, fallen in love with her, although certainly not, I quickly told myself, in a sexual way.

She was more like the sister I'd always wanted, as opposed to the two I had, both more than ten years my senior, who whispered and giggled together in an impenetrable twosome and even now treated me like a silly kid.

Suza didn't give the impression of taking trouble over her appearance, but she had a heavy sensuality about her, like a musky perfume, and I knew it would draw a man to her if and when she decided she wanted one. Now, in early October, she wore the remains of a deep summer tan, running from her face, down her neck and shoulders and into the generous shadow of her breasts in a mulberry-coloured velvet sweater.

She looked good in reds and purples, in yellows and golds, in bold, regal colours, not in the self-effacing blues and greys that I wore, little different from my school uniform.

"What sort of men do you find attractive?" I asked. "When you're in the mood?"

"Oh . . . dark, skinny, neurotic: half the men I fancy disappear into the sunset muttering that their mother wouldn't like them to get mixed up with a shiksa."

I told her about me and Don, because she seemed genuinely interested: how we'd met in summer rep at Eastbourne in 1970 when he was twenty-two and I was twenty-one, when he was a rude mechanical and I was a fairy one week, and we were those hateful, bottled-up, middle-aged creatures in *Dangerous Corner* the next, with hefty make-up and grey powder in our hair.

The play changed on Wednesday since the holidaymakers came and went at the weekend and that way we could drag them in twice.

It was rare for a member of the audience to be under sixty. We convinced ourselves it was invaluable experience. It could have been worse: we could have the spent the summer as Red Coats at Butlins in bracing Skegness.

"I thought at first that he was gay," I remembered.

"Andy!"

"He had a lot of gay friends. It hadn't been legal long and they liked to camp it up, especially in Eastbourne which was so staid; that old-fashioned *bonar palare* stuff. *Épater* the bourgeoisie. You know, I've come to the conclusion that he liked women to think he was gay; that way he was a challenge to them and he could sit back and let them seduce him. He always was lazy!"

"It proves that adage," Suza said, "that the ones who're most sure of their sexuality are most at ease with gays. The queer-bashers are the ones who're afraid they might be tempted. My ex was a great one for sneering at pansies, faggots, woofters. Then two days after his thirty-third birthday he gets himself arrested for cottaging in a public lavatory in Acton – some sort of birthday present to himself, presumably. I ask you, *Acton*! What sort of man can you possibly pick up there?"

"You wouldn't have minded so much if it'd been Chiswick?"

"Well, quite. Much better class of rough trade." She looked at me dispassionately for a moment. "Tell me,

Jennifer. Have you never wondered what it would be like with another man?"

"Yes," I admitted. "Occasionally, in the abstract. But then I figured it would probably be pretty much the same. I mean, I've read books and seen films – and I don't believe half of what happens in *them*." I studied my fingernails, feeling my cheeks redden. "And how different can it be when – ultimately, at the end of any amount of faffing about – the same something ends up in the same somewhere?"

So, why are men so quick to stray?

She began to laugh. "You know something, Jenny? You're damn right. It *is* pretty much the same. Bloody boring! Who needs it?"

"Clearly I'm an idiot savant," I said drily. "Or is that only *half* right?"

"Tell me more about Eastbourne. It sounds exotic."

"Hardly! We acted all the old warhorses that season." That rainy Sussex summer that seemed to last for ever because I was so much in love.

"We never got to do any new plays," I said. "Want to put bums on seats? Do Coward and Rattigan. Find a potboiler. Do *Gaslight*."

"That rings a bell. I know: the one about the man who sets out to drive his wife mad? I've seen the film."

"That's it. I think I can remember some of my lines from that. Mind you, I was only the tarty maid. '*I beg yer pardon. I fought the bell rung.*'"

Don was the wicked husband; he enjoyed that. Julie

Smallbone was his long-suffering wife. I got to kiss him in the second act when I told him his wife was "a pore thing, sir" and he'd be better off with me. He had a caddish moustache and it tickled.

I remember the way we grinned at each other as we flung out our lines. The rest of the cast didn't know our secret. One afternoon, as he took me in his arms, I felt his erection pressing against my belly. It was the most either of us could do to keep straight faces and I got off stage as fast as I could, forgetting the tray I was supposed to take.

I remember how surprised everyone looked at the end-of-season party when Don announced our big news and our director said, "Well, what a pair of dark horses you are!"

Suza refilled both our glasses, tipping up the bottle of rough red wine by the neck with gusto, and finally slapped the greasy sandwiches onto the kitchen table.

"Cheers."

Spots of melting butter and bacon fat oozed onto the plate. I picked the sandwich up and tackled it, leaning well forward so I wouldn't get marks on my cardigan. I felt grease trickle down my chin.

"Would moddom care for some Daddy's Sauce?" Suza asked. I shook my head. She poured the brown stuff lavishly onto her plate.

"*Bon appetit.*"

# Learning the lines

Don had landed a role as guest star in a long-running detective series. It was only one episode but it was a big part and required both location work in Yorkshire and studio work in London. He was a baddie and got to kill somebody, which he enjoys. He was pleased with himself which meant that life went smoothly and everyone was happy: him, me, his agent and our pet accountant.

He started to make love to me again. Being out of work struck at his libido, just when you'd think he would have the time and energy to enjoy a long lecherous lie-in. Getting a good meaty role pumped up his hormones and put an end to the fallow period.

After twenty-five years we knew what suited us both and weren't inclined to experiment. At least it didn't seem that he'd been learning new tricks from old dogs. It was pretty good, as it always had been. He was more affectionate when the sex was regular.

In fact he took me to Bruges for the weekend on the Felixstowe – Zeebrugge ferry while Suza came in to feed the dogs. We'd gone there when we were young and poor and newly married, when it was all we could afford, and I had happy memories of strolling by the canals, making believe we were in Venice, eating *steack-frites* in tiny family bistros.

"Do you love me?" I asked him one morning in our dark hotel room.

"You know I do."

"But you never say it."

"I shouldn't need to." I was lying on my stomach and he rolled over and slapped my bottom, hard. "I love you, Jennifer. Okay?"

Okay.

He was going to be away for four days in Scarborough and made an early start on Monday morning to get there in time – early as in five a.m. He could have driven up the previous day, of course, and stayed an extra night at their expense, and the fact that he declined to do so pleased me.

We spent the last night he was at home quietly eating by candlelight, then sharing a bath in our big round tub – one of our few domestic extravagances – then an early night.

I offered to get up to make breakfast but he said he couldn't eat anything that early and would stop at a roadside caff on his way.

"Sure you'll be okay?" he asked as he came to give me a last kiss goodbye in the darkness.

"Aren't I always?"

"I'll give you a ring tomorrow night."

"Fine. Drive safely."

I turned over and moved back towards sleep. I heard the creaking of the five-bar gate two minutes later and the swish of the gravel as the car drove out and revved northwards. He couldn't be bothered to get out of the car and close the gate behind him. Aggie began to bark but I knew she'd stop if I ignored her.

I was looking forward to four days on my own, pottering about, eating leftovers, walking the dogs. And if I got lonely, I could ask Suza to come and stay the night.

There was a frost that morning, so unseasonable was the weather, and I found myself wishing it would warm up again. Clearly somebody up there was listening, since that was the night the house caught fire.

# Fire!

I went to bed feeling hard done by. Suza had announced that she was going up to London for the day to have lunch with her agent and an editor who was trying to poach her away from her existing publisher with offers of what seemed like fantastic sums of money. She might, she added, stay overnight if there was anything good on in the West End.

I hadn't heard from her and assumed that she'd done just that. Worse, Don had broken his promise to ring me that evening. I could already hear his excuses: how the whole unit had been in the pub until well after chucking-out time, how they'd then raided the minibar in someone's hotel room, how it then been 'far too late after all that to disturb you, darling'.

He keeps a studio photo of himself on his study wall, taken twenty years ago. Vain thing. When he's away I take it down and keep it by me, in the sitting room or next to the bed. I have to remember to put it back before his return or he'll think I'm silly.

We keep the bedroom door shut at night because

the dogs, unlike Don, think that five o'clock in the morning is a good time to eat breakfast. When he's away I usually turn the key too. I don't know why I bother: the house isn't within earshot of anywhere else and the Mad Axeman, should he turn up, could kick the door down at his leisure.

Why not use his axe on it, you ask? So as to keep the edge keen for my neck.

I woke up from a deep sleep to the barking of Scamper at my door. I can distinguish with ease the two dogs' voices. There was a note of panic in her yapping and she was scrabbling at the wooden panels with her claws.

I could see the digital LED display on my clock radio and it said 2.17, which was a very early breakfast, even for Scamper. I rolled out of bed. I was wearing a red winceyette nightie and an old pair of Don's woollen socks with a hole in the heel. This outfit is warm and I wear it when he isn't there to see it and be turned off by it.

I could smell burning as soon as I left the room. I hesitated at the top of the stairs; I think I contemplated for a moment going back to bed and pulling the covers over my head. There was a phone by the bed and I could have rung for the fire brigade but it seemed more important to throw on a raincoat and wellingtons and get out of the house if real danger threatened.

Oddly, I felt calm. I moved down the wooden treads, aware of how cold my bare heel was, and followed my nose into the sitting room. The first thing I saw was Aggie, crouched behind the sofa, whining. She'd always been afraid of fire. I hadn't switched the light on but I hardly needed to; in front of the grate the hearthrug was well ablaze, shedding a dancing light on the room.

I picked up the vase of late roses I'd carefully arranged that morning, wrenched the flowers out and flung the water over the rug. It sizzled and partly subsided. I ran to the kitchen and filled two large jugs from the tap and finished the job. I picked up the ruined rug and bundled it out into the glory hole by the back door – that repository of homeless bric-a-brac.

"Good riddance," I muttered, since I'd never liked the rug, a gift from my late mother-in-law. I slammed the door of the glory hole shut again. I went back into the sitting room and switched on the light. Aggie emerged from behind the sofa, looking bashful. Scamper sat where the rug had been, panting slightly. I stroked her head.

"Good girl," I said. "Good girl. And a fat lot of use you are in an emergency, Aggie Donleavy!"

The carpet in front of the fireplace was charred but a new rug would disguise that. Luckily the curtains and loose covers were some distance away and wouldn't have caught for a while, after which the whole house would have gone up in a matter of minutes. Fire regulations, Don had told the surveyor fifteen years ago. Who gives a toss about fire regulations when they're not retrospective?

I'd lit a fire in the grate last night, partly because it was cold and partly to enliven my solitude with its cosy flickering. I was sure that I'd put the fireguard up before going to bed.

Wasn't I?

I'd been fuming at Don for not calling. I'd had a stiff brandy by way of a nightcap. Could second nature for once have failed? But the fireguard lay on the hearth, on its side, not upright against the chimney breast where it would have been had I simply forgotten about it.

I looked sternly at Scamper. "Maybe you're not such a good girl after all!"

Clearly the dogs had crept out of the kitchen during the night in search of some warmth, curled up by the fire and somebody – some overeager puppy – had swiped the fireguard aside with her wanton tail, allowing a last dying coal to jump free and flare.

"Well, no harm done," I said aloud. I would shut the dogs in the kitchen at night from now on. I would douse the fire before I retired to bed. You couldn't be too careful.

When Don rang the next morning with the dialogue I'd written for him, I tried my best to make a drama out of the incident; but having established that a) I was unhurt, b) the dogs were unhurt and c) the house was undamaged, my husband wouldn't indulge my histrionics. In search of more generous company I walked down to Madder Cottage.

# Humility

I was surprised, crossing the green, to notice someone coming out of the church. Normally it's kept locked except when a service is taking place. I hurried over. I didn't know the woman, possibly a tourist; she took no notice of me but got into a green hatchback and drove away.

It's the Church of St James the Less: galling for him, you would think, but no doubt it's a lesson in humility.

I pushed at the church door and it yielded to my touch. A youngish woman in dungarees looked up as I came in. She wore large red-framed spectacles that magnified her eyes. She had a box full of cleaning materials with her and a broom.

"Getting a lot of visitors today," she said. "Two in five minutes. Unheard of."

"I happened to see that the church was open."

It was the vicar's wife, I realised, his second wife since he'd divorced the first and married this – much younger – woman who'd been one of his parishioners. She wasn't pretty and made no attempt to enhance even the little that nature had given her, but no doubt it was their souls that had merged over their shared faith. It was a nine-day wonder in the parish but if the bishop could wear it, so could we. I couldn't remember her name now, although it had been on everyone's lips at the time.

It was hard to tell under the dungarees but I thought she was faintly pregnant. Go forth and multiply. They lived in a modern bungalow on the outskirts of one of the larger villages that made up his parish, so much easier to manage than a huge Victorian rectory.

"I thought the place could do with a dusting," she explained. "I try to get round them all regularly but it's a thankless task."

"Not long till Harvest Festival," I remarked.

"Oh! Don't talk to me about Harvest Festival!"

"You don't mind if I . . ."

"Not at all." She gestured. "Be my guest."

I'd never been in the church when it was silent and empty like this. I walked towards the altar to admire the carved screenwork.

"The twelve apostles." The woman's voice close behind me made me jump. I hadn't heard her approach and saw now that she wore house shoes, almost slippers. Clearly she was the sort who can never leave anyone alone. "Isn't it marvellous? Look at Judas, at the end there, out on a limb, his head and body turned away from the others. I believe it's unique for such a screen to include him: the outcast."

The greatest traitor in history, the man who sold his

best friend; yet surely he was only doing his duty. "What a pity the church can't be open more often," I said.

"Yes," she agreed. "But it isn't safe. There are people whose idea of fun would be to wreck this priceless screen, not for any monetary gain for themselves but out of sheer . . ." She paused, seeking the appropriate word, then clearly found it. "Devilment." Her plain, jolly face was serious now.

"Do you believe in the devil?" I asked.

She replied simply, "Of course. How can I believe in God and not the Devil?" Unless, I thought, they are the same person. "Have you seen the bells?" she asked. "The inscription is rather nice, I always think. It's not locked."

I went into the bell tower and slowly climbed the rickety stairs. We had four bells and each had a line inscribed round its base. Together they read:

> Glad do I ring the joyous day
> when man and wife unite
> to pledge today and evermore
> their happy nuptial rite.

Today and evermore: presumably the vicar's first wife had expected those words to mean something.

# A journey

Don's car was in the garage, having an emergency operation, so I drove him to the station to catch the train to London for some studio filming to complete the Scarborough work on the detective series.

He would stay for a couple of nights at the flat of an old LAMDA friend in Covent Garden. Toby Richards had recently been noticed by Hollywood and was away indefinitely in LA being a tight-lipped English villain in a series of action movies starring people like Bruce Willis and Sylvester Stallone, a fact of which Don was studiously unenvious while trying not to grind his teeth.

Two or three of Toby's friends had keys to the place and were told they were welcome to use it whenever they liked, to keep away burglars and squatters. I did wonder what would happen if more than one old friend availed himself of this invitation on the same night, especially if accompanied by a woman not his wife, but that hadn't happened so far or if it had I hadn't heard about it.

They were digging up the road near the station and we arrived with less than five minutes to spare. If it'd been up to me, I'd have set off earlier but Don thought he was too important to hang around at provincial railway stations waiting on British Rail.

"Don't bother to park," he said, leaning over – not to kiss me goodbye, as I initially thought, but to grab his overnight bag from the back seat.

"It's no trouble." There was a vacant space right in front of the ticket office so I defiantly backed into it and we both got out. He flashed his American Express card at the man in uniform, signed the slip and strode onto the London platform, which wasn't crowded, rush hour being long over.

One person I did see at the far end of the platform, to my surprise, was Suza. She stood with her hands thrust into her coat pockets, a small suitcase clutched tightly between her ankles. She looked thoughtful, not smiling to herself as she often did in repose.

"Look," I said. "It's Suza."

Don glanced up the platform. "Oh, yes. So it is. Hope she's not going all the way up to London."

"Where else would she be going?"

I called out to my friend and she turned and waved but made no attempt to join us. I moved up the platform towards her with Don trailing reluctantly in my wake.

"Suza," I said. "Where on earth are you off to?"

"I had a call from an old neighbour in Hammersmith," she said. "Her mother's had a stroke and she's in a bit of a state. We weren't bosom buddies but we were quite friendly and I said I'd go and keep her company, boost her morale, help with the practical problems. Hello, Andy."

"Hello."

"You didn't tell me," I said, hurt. I'd told her I wouldn't be able to make lunch that day precisely because I was driving Don to the station and stopping off in town after to do a little shopping.

"It was so sudden, Jenny. I didn't know I was going until half an hour ago. I just had time to chuck a few things into a case and make it to the station for the eleven twenty-five. I'm sorry. I'd have given you a ring from London."

"Don's going up to town too," I said, taking his arm. "You can travel together."

"That'll be nice," Don said, selecting an eager anticipatory look from his repertoire of faces and gluing it on.

I don't think Suza was taken in by this, as she smiled a subtle smile. "You not going, Jenny?"

"No, it's work, not pleasure."

"Not both?" she asked.

"Certainly not," Don said.

"I'd have told you if I'd been going too." I heard my voice, a little cold. "If I was going to be away." I saw the electric train with its snub nose appear in the distance. The track was straight and it was visible long before it was audible. I watched it glide silently towards us.

"Here we are," I said cheerfully. I glanced at my watch. "Bang on time." I embraced Don hard, unselfconscious in front of Suza for whom it was no news that I was indecently in love with my husband. He, however, looked embarrassed, glancing at her as if in the hope that she hadn't noticed our public display of affection. He ended the hug before it had properly begun, deftly disentangling himself.

"Ring me, darling," I said.

"I'll try."

I kissed Suza too, on the cheek. "Hope everything works out for your friend."

"I'm sure the situation will resolve itself," she said, "one way or another. That is to say that the old lady will either recover or die."

They got into the same carriage. They could hardly, I thought with amusement, have done otherwise. I waved them goodbye.

# Something useful

To my surprise Don rang me every evening while he was away. On the fourth day I went to fetch him at the station. He looked tired but contented. He hugged me hard, unselfconsciously, in public, and said that he had missed me and that it was good to be home.

We had a quiet evening in. I did his laundry, then sat with him before a log fire. I caught him looking at me once or twice, his face concerned. Then he would smile, the corners of his mouth turning up so swiftly and easily that I wondered if I'd imagined it. "What's up?" I would say and he would reply, "Nothing! Why should there be?"

I didn't believe him. That's one of the big problems with being married to an actor: you know the heights of insincerity of which they're capable. I've seen him swear undying love, most convincingly, to a woman he could scarcely bring himself to speak to off stage. At least there was no chance of him really falling for that bitch, which is something that worries me. It's the ultimate proof of behavioural therapy: when you act being in love with someone, displaying all the symptoms, then there's a danger you will come to believe yourself so.

As the famous director said, when asked if Hamlet and Ophelia had an affair, "In my productions, always!"

Finally, he put down his copy of *Casting News* and said to me, "Jennifer, have you ever considered going back to work?"

"Work?" I echoed stupidly. "What sort of work?"

He looked mildly impatient. "Acting, Jennifer. It's what you do, remember? Drama school, Eastbourne rep, five lines in *Coronation Street* as one of Ken Barlow's innumerable girlfriends."

"No," I said quickly. "I hadn't thought of it. Why? We don't need the money." He earned enough and both sets of parents had left us a bit. There were no children to support through school and university.

"It's not a matter of money," he said, "but of you, of your mental health. I've been a bit worried about you lately." I must have looked startled, even indignant, because he went on hastily, "You're alone an awful lot, Jen. You're too wrapped up in your dogs and your garden. Little things assume a disproportionate importance, like that dying ember on the fireside rug, that would have burnt itself out in a few minutes, but which you make out to be akin to the Great Fire of Windsor Castle—"

"I'm not alone," I butted in. "I've got Suza—"

"Suza agrees with me—"

"You've been *discussing* me with Suza!" I heard my

voice rising, like hysteria. "The two of you have discussed me behind my back?"

I wasn't sure whose betrayal I minded most.

His face was so filled with concern now that I wanted to slap it out of him. "She thinks you need more occupation too."

"I see! You mean she's bored with me coming round all the time."

"That's not what she means at all. She's fond of you. She loves having your company but she agrees with me that everybody should have something useful to do."

I couldn't speak: so I was useless now.

He passed the copy of the news-sheet to me. "Look in here. Auditions for a new contemporary drama. They want all ages and types. You've kept up your Equity membership. Why not give it a try? What have you got to lose? Get some representation."

I took the paper from him, but didn't open it. It hung limply in my fingers. I couldn't now remember why I'd ever wanted to be an actor in the first place. My aunts had been surprised. Jennifer? But she's such a shy creature. That was the whole point, I suppose: on stage I wasn't clumsy Jennifer Farrell but someone else, someone glamorous and bold.

"Sid Daley is dead," I said. "Remember? We went to the funeral."

A sweet monster of a man; they had to burn him in an extra-large coffin.

"There are other agents!"

"Sure! Desperate to take on a middle-aged never-was, in a time when they can't find work for the actresses over forty they've already got on their books. Contemporary drama? A soap opera, in other words."

"There's nothing like a sudsa for making you a household name," he pointed out, "After which the world's yer lobster."

I took refuge in sarcasm. "I suppose I could answer one of those ads for "dancing girls" they have at the back of *The Stage* . . . Oh, no. I forgot. I'm not tall enough."

"Maybe for a tour to the Far East," he said lightly, "where people are shorter." He hates rows and tries to head one off with a joke. This can infuriate when there are times, such as now, when I feel the need for a good shouting match. "You were good, Jen," he said softly. "Much better than me, if truth be told."

I stared, astonished at this admission, which was unprecedented, disarming me as the joke could not. The gospel according to Don Donleavy was that no one was better than Don Donleavy.

# Blood flowing

I assumed that we'd have children because that was what married couples did. Obviously there was no hurry as we were both so young. In fact, we talked about it before the wedding and Don said firmly that we wouldn't even think about it for five years by which time we would, of course, be established, even famous: sought after by producers and agents, he playing Hamlet to my Ophelia at the RSC with a bit of Hollywood-film money in the bank. Burton and Taylor, Olivier and Leigh, Donleavy and Farrell.

It didn't work out like that, of course, it seldom does; but after seven or eight years we were making a decent living – TV bit parts, a few weeks' rep, the occasional supporting role in the West End, adverts – and with him turning thirty and me already twenty-nine, we decided that it was probably time to reproduce ourselves.

Except that it didn't work out like that either. Two or three years went by, with the regular flow of blood disappointing my hopes. I became more and more keen on the idea of becoming a mother, as any unreachable fruit seems more succulent.

Eventually we went for tests and received the devastating news that it was unlikely Don would ever father a child. Hard hearing for any man, a cruel blow to his virility. Eight years I'd been on the pill, suffering water retention and weight gain and even an outbreak of gruesome spots on my back at one point, and I needn't have bothered.

I suppose a good many marriages break up at this point as the wife seeks a partner who can give her children before it's too late and the husband is too unmanned to put up a fight; but I honestly don't think it occurred to me that I might leave Don. He mattered more to me than any hypothetical baby.

Not that I didn't take it hard; I suppose we both did. We didn't make love for months after, I remember, as his confidence reeled from the wound, while to me there seemed no point. It was at this stage that I gave up my career, stopped ringing my agent or even answering his calls. What was the good of looking for work when getting out of a chair took all my strength and will-power?

Depression is a strange thing. My doctor was sympathetic, all the doctors I saw during those months were. I came from a family that didn't succumb to unhappiness, that put a brave face on and made the best of it. Such things are deeply engrained in the soul, making it hard to ask for help when it's needed. And if a pill can make you feel better merely by altering the chemical balance in your brain, doesn't that mean that emotions, feelings, even passions – that they aren't real?

Don worked harder than ever and it wasn't long after this that he told me he was going for an audition for 'some crazy new ITV thing set in space' and came home a few weeks later as Captain Will Davenant of the *Bounty*.

It was that night, after he heard that he'd got the part, and a promise of more money than he'd earned in a long time, that he turned to me again, taking me in his arms, kissing me, stroking my breasts, my buttocks, whispering into my ear, like the old days.

"We have each other, Jenny."

"Yes, darling. Yes."

I think now that childless couples are closer, more intimate, than the rest.

# Jealousy

"So you and Don have discussed me and found me idle."

Suza stood back from the vase of chrysanthemums she was arranging – white ones with yellow eyes. She might not be able to cook but she had the knack with flowers and they fell into disciplined place at her touch. She had her hair back this morning, caught in a soft knot at the nape of her neck. Her face looked bare but pure and noble.

"I think you should elucidate that remark," she said.

I did so and she looked at me, bemused. Apparently satisfied with her arrangement at last, she stood the vase on the table between two half-burnt white candles. I wondered if she ate alone by candlelight in the evening, or if she was preparing a sacrifice.

A quiet moment or two passed before she answered me, as if she was collecting her thoughts. "What happened was that I was asking Andy about your acting career in the train, more for something to say than anything else. I didn't want to bolster his ego by inciting him to talk about *his* career. He said that you'd been good, which surprised me."

"Well, thanks."

"I mean I was surprised that he should say so. He strikes me as the sort of man who likes to keep his wife in her place: one step behind."

"Undermining my self-esteem, as they say in the women's magazines?"

"Well, yes. Anyway, I said in that case it was pity you'd given it up. That was all. End of conversation. Change of subject to the beauty of the East Anglian landscape and the prospects of the new Labour government. But you seem to have no difficulty in filling your time, Jenny, what with walking the dogs, tending your lovely garden, making your wonderful cakes and jam and so on."

It sounded unutterably dreary when she put it like that but her voice had the ring of sincerity in it.

"I'm surprised he should so have misrepresented my views," she went on. "I wonder sometimes . . ."

"What?" It was too late for her to stop now.

"If he isn't jealous of our friendship, wanting to drive a wedge between us."

"Oh, surely he's glad to see me make a friend. You credit him with being more manipulative than he is." I almost said *even* more manipulative.

"You're an innocent in some ways," she said. "I've seen more of life than you have. I've seen men ready to kill to defend the status quo."

"Perhaps he *is* afraid of you," I said. "He knows you don't think much of him."

She protested this point, though clearly more out of duty than anything. "I think he takes you too much for granted," she conceded. "Mind you," she continued, "I don't think a woman should be too dependent on a man."

"You think I'm too emotionally dependent on Don?"

"I was thinking more of straightforward financial dependence, actually. I mean, what if he were to fall under a bus tomorrow?"

"Or leave me for another woman?"

"I wasn't going to say that."

"Why, what have you heard?"

"Absolutely nothing!"

"If he falls under a bus," I said, "I have him well insured."

## Two by two

I decided to hold a dinner party to celebrate Don's forty-ninth birthday on October the twenty-fourth, which happened to be a Friday. Who would be the guests? I wanted Suza along, obviously, and there was room for a maximum of eight with comfort at our dining table.

I toyed with the idea of making it a surprise party but gave it up in the end as too impractical. Don would be bound to spot the preparations and it would be better if he chose the wine. I'd never been any good at keeping secrets, especially from him.

I didn't want to invite any of our London friends as we would be obliged to ask them for the whole weekend and I didn't feel up to that sort of company at the moment.

I settled on Bill and Penny Gammon, a couple in their mid-fifties to whom we owed hospitality. I also invited the Crosses, who were in their late thirties and had a barn conversion in the next village but lived in a flat in the Barbican all week, since they were both Something in the City. I hardly knew them but thought they would be pleased enough to meet a famous author and a semi-famous actor, which it seemed they were as they accepted at once.

Don thought I ought to invite an extra man for Suza, to "make up the numbers", but I vetoed this idea as hopelessly old-fashioned.

"It's not as if we're going to have a wife-swapping orgy after dinner," I pointed out.

"I'm glad to hear it. I don't fancy Penny Bacon—"

"You know perfectly well that her name is Gammon!"

"—at all. She's got a face like a pig . . . Quite appropriate when you come to think of it." We both giggled, me guiltily since Penny Gammon was a kind and generous woman, if no oil painting. Like many beautiful people Don is faintly contemptuous of the ill-favoured, as if they do it on purpose. "And I don't like the sound of Claire Cross, either," he went on. "Yuppie type."

"She's pretty, as it happens, and very elegant. You must have seen her around. She drives a white Golf GTi convertible. Most of the men round here look twice."

"But as hard as nails. I know the sort."

"I think yuppies died out in the recession," I said. "Anyway, we've settled that there is no earthly need for the animals to go in two by two. Besides, I don't want Suza to think I'm trying to fix her up with someone. That would be crass. She might take offence."

Actually, she never took offence. She said either people were trying deliberately to be rude to you, in which case the best thing was to laugh it off, or they were stupid and insensitive, in which case the best thing was to laugh it off.

And the only single male I could think of off-hand was Mr Herzog who was over seventy.

Suza, however, was less than enthusiastic when I told her about the dinner. "They'll ask me where I get my ideas from," she complained. "You know I'm not sociable, Jenny. A regular recluse, me. That's why I decided to leave the crowds of London and lose myself in the country."

"Please," I said, since it suddenly seemed important that Suza should be at the party, as if it was in her honour and not Don's. "Pretty please. I want to make it a nice evening for Don."

She raised her eyebrows. "And my being there will ensure that?"

"It's his birthday," I said, sidestepping this question, "and next year he'll be fifty. He hates getting old."

"I can't think why. What does he do now that he won't be able to do when he's seventy-five? Come to that, what did he do when he was twenty-five that he can't do now?"

"He used to play a bit of tennis in those days," I said, choosing to take the question seriously, "but he wasn't much good at it."

She laughed. "So long as a man can get it up he's usually satisfied with the exercise he's getting." Her eyes twinkled. "I take it Andy *can* still get it up?"

"Mmm. Of course."

"Well, that's all right, then."

"I think ageing must be hard for beautiful people," I went on humbly. "Much harder than for the rest of us who have so much less to lose."

"You do yourself down too much, Jenny." She lifted my hair from my neck and coiled it in elegant folds on my head. It was weeks since I'd had it cut and it looked a mess. "You have a fine, mature figure," she said, "and good thick hair, and a sweet, pretty face."

"Mature! Thanks."

"A woman is at her best in her middle years, when she is more sure of herself, less self-conscious."

"I'm not," I said. "Less self-conscious. Inside I feel like a gauche eighteen-year-old."

"Look at me," she said. "I've got jodhpur thighs and wrinkles and plenty of grey hair. And I figure any man who gets to go to bed with me should be thanking God on his knees for his good luck."

"I wish I was more like you."

"Don't wish that," she said. "All you need to be is your sweet self." She kissed me. "You'll look lovely at the party. You'll see. We'll have a girls' day out in London a few days before. I'll take you to a hairdresser I know in Kensington who'll invent a more flattering cut for you; and we'll get some low-lights put in to give it a coppery glow. Then we'll choose you a new outfit."

"I feel funny about spending money on myself."

"Nuts. Raid the joint bank account. Andy can afford it,

can't he? Or is he one of these Neanderthal husbands who don't tell their wives how much they earn?"

"Hardly! Who do you think keeps the books for the accountant and does the VAT returns? The dogs?"

"You can say in a way it's for his benefit. We'll give you a real makeover and you must be an expert in cosmetics with your acting training so you'll be the belle of the ball. How does that sound?"

"It sounds like you're coming to the dinner."

"Yes," she replied with a laugh. "You've trapped me. I guess I'm coming. I'd walk many miles for your cooking, anyhow, and endure any number of bores."

I wondered if she included Don in that category.

## The man who fell

"Have you ever played a gay man?" Suza asked.

"No." Don looked apologetic. "Or not on film or TV, anyway. I've always turned down such . . . opportunities. It's just that some people have difficulty distinguishing the man from the part and I feel it wouldn't do my image as a gorgeous sex god any good."

"Have you ever taken your clothes off on stage or on film?" she went on.

"No, but then I've never been asked. I'm not opposed to it in principle, or wouldn't have been when I was younger. I have nothing to be ashamed of."

"I'm glad no one ever asked me to strip," I said. "Or should I be insulted?" Although I knew women who'd made porn films to pay the rent, or feed a drug habit, and not always soft porn either. I'd probably been lucky.

"Modesty is a fine thing in a woman," my husband said with a grin. "Especially in a wife."

"You did that sex scene in *The Man Who Fell*," I reminded him.

"Oh? When was this?" Suza asked.

"1978," I said.

"I wasn't actually naked for that," he pointed out.

"It looked as though you were, though," I said, "on screen. And—" I turned to Suza "—he had to fondle some girl's breasts – what was her name, darling? – and kiss them."

"Yes, it was sheer hell," he said cheerfully, "but I'm dedicated to my art. And her name was Wendy Sotherby. Perfectly nice woman. I must say I found the Sellotape on her nipples a bit off-putting. Don't ask!"

"So were you he?" Suza asked. "The Man Who Fell?"

"No, I was his best friend, and I was screwing his wife."

"An interesting definition of best friend," she said, "and is it out on video?"

"No," Don said firmly.

"The fan club has some pirate copies," I said, "taped from satellite TV."

"You know what I think about pirate videos," Don said. "That's my bread and butter being stolen there, and everyone else's."

I demurred. "Not if the film isn't otherwise available, surely."

"It's the principle of the thing," he said, putting on his most priggish look. I realised that he didn't want Suza to see him even virtually naked.

# Wise virgins

Suza and I got off the train together three evenings later, giggling like two of the unwise virgins who've discovered their oil has run out. I felt as if I'd been on holiday. I gathered up a clutch of bags from Harvey Nichols and we made for the car park and Suza's Land-rover.

"Are you coming in for a cup of tea?" I asked when we drew up outside my house. "I know I'm parched."

"Okay," she said, "I'll come in for a few minutes." She killed the engine and helped me extract my shopping from the back.

The clocks would go back that Sunday and it was already dark. A shaft of light fell across us and I saw that Don had the door open, having heard our scrunching on the gravel. The dogs ran out to bark an excited greeting and I realised how seldom I was away from home for longer than it took to go to the supermarket.

I staggered into the house under the weight of my purchases, while Suza floated behind me with nothing but her capacious shoulder bag swinging from her arm. She'd bought precisely nothing for herself.

Don whistled, seeing me clearly for the first time. He said to Suza, "Who is this gorgeous creature? Didn't you have my wife with you when you left this morning?"

"She's always been gorgeous," Suza said. "You just stopped noticing."

"Not so."

"You better keep an eye on her, Andy, or she'll be running off with some man who appreciates her."

"*I* appreciate her."

"Do you really like it?" I asked.

"I like it very much," he said, which convinced me more than superlatives could. On our wedding day I asked him if he thought it was true that all brides were beautiful and he answered simply, "I only know that you are."

I'd had a wonderful time at the hairdressers, which was also a beauticians. Marcus, who flattered and flirted nonstop, but like he meant it, had transformed my mousy tresses. I'd long worn my hair swept back off my forehead in a style I now saw was slightly severe. He'd given me a wispy fringe that took five years off my age. But first he deftly wrapped strands of my hair in tinfoil, removing them later to reveal copper streaks that looked perfectly natural but made me generally more glamorous, more *dangerous*. The new red locks fell in the faintest of curls to my collar.

A girl called Trish had manicured me while Marcus did his work, smoothing the garden-roughened nails and French polishing them, as I wondered how long they would last like that with the dead-heading to do. I then had a facial and an eyelash tint, seeing my normally pale cheeks glowing with health, my eyes suddenly wider and bluer.

For three hours they fetched me tea, coffee, the latest magazines, even offering smoked-salmon sandwiches and a glass of champagne. Suza sat all that time with infinite patience, giving an opinion when asked and keeping quiet when not. Occasionally she gossiped scandalously with Marcus about people they both knew and I wondered, not for the first time, why she'd left this glittering life for the mud of Suffolk.

I was treated like a queen and the correspondingly regal size of the bill made me blink; but then I thought, What the hell, he can afford it.

We had a late lunch in the restaurant on the top floor of Harvey Nicks, then spent the rest of the afternoon combing the place, with frequent forays to Harrods and even Browns, until we'd decided on exactly the right outfit for the new Jennifer Donleavy's inaugural dinner party.

"I'll put the kettle on," I said, happy enough to come down to earth.

"Not for me," Suza said. "I must go and do some work – earn an honest crust. I only came in to see Andy's reaction."

"And did you find my performance convincing?" he asked sardonically.

"Oh yes," she said. "It was worthy of a BAFTA."

# Blue pasta

"Is it my imagination, Jennifer," Penny Gammon said, "or a trick of the light, or is this pasta blue?"

"It's tagliatelle flavoured with seaweed," I explained.

"Sure it hasn't gorn orf?" Bill Gammon asked, rolling his eyes, making everyone laugh.

"It's simply delicious," Claire Cross said dutifully, although I noticed she'd eaten little of it. Claire was as thin and angular as a giraffe and I suspected that she hadn't got that way by eating lots of pasta in creamy prawn sauce.

Suza smiled at me in silent support and gave me the suspicion of a wink.

I'd had a moment of panic that morning, wondering if my ill-assorted guests could possibly meld into a successful dinner party; but I was bored with meals where everyone was in the same line of business and talked shop all evening. Penny Gammon always looked as if she was wearing tweeds with the skirt seated even when, as now, she'd got her best Liberty frock and pearls on. Claire Cross had dressed down in black leggings and a silk blouse that might be see-through in some lights. They barely seemed to belong to the same species.

Now, halfway through the first course, I was optimistic. Everyone had complimented me on my appearance, even old Bill Gammon who, I'd imagined, never noticed that sort of thing. My new Annabel Wu dress was black silk jersey, fiendishly simple, shift-like to the hips, then swinging in well-cut folds to below the knee. It disguised quite brilliantly any excess flab around the thighs or waist. My copper-coloured jacket shimmered in the candlelight, picking up and enhancing the new colour of my hair. I'd been afraid to tell Don how much it cost but he hadn't asked. It may simply not have occurred to him that such a plain outfit could be pushing our credit card to its limit this month.

Suza had come round specially that morning, not to offer help with the food as I'd feared, but to give me the most beautiful pair of long copper earrings which now cascaded barbarically from my lobes. She claimed she'd happened to see them in an African craft shop and that they'd cost next to nothing, but I didn't believe a word of it.

I'd finished my starter and lifted my glass of Sancerre to my lips, enjoying the slippery taste of it as I surveyed my table. Suza was on my immediate right with Bill next to her and Claire Cross to his right. Tim Cross sat on my left with Penny Gammon between him and Don, the birthday boy, who sat enthroned in splendour at the head of the table. He was wearing the cream silk suit he'd had run up for him in Hong Kong when he was filming there five years ago and which seemed set to last a lifetime.

He was flirting gamely with Penny, who was observing this phenomenon with amused detachment, finally turning to me and calling down the table, "You should put this husband of yours on the stage, Jenny. He's as good as a play."

I saw a look of puzzlement settle across Tim's bland features. "I thought you *were* on the stage," he said. Everyone looked at him. "Oh," he said. "Joke. I get it."

Suza needn't have worried that the Crosses would ask her where she got her ideas from. Tim Cross was interested enough in her profession but, it turned out, solely from a financial point of view. He asked some pretty personal questions about what sort of advance an author of Suza's stature could hope to command, questions which I, her best friend, would have blushed to put. Suza answered him with equanimity.

The Crosses had thirteen-year-old twin boys – that being presumably the most efficient way of breeding a family. They were at the same boarding school, in the same class, as Prince Harry. They liked to let people know this. "Poor little chap," Tim said solicitously, having brought the subject up. "Been through the most ghastly time recently. Can you imagine?" We murmured politely.

I cleared the first course and brought in an array of dishes and warm plates, while Don went round refilling everyone's glass. Claire Cross continued to toy with her food, which I found mildly irritating, longing to tell her, as my mother had me in my youth, that there were children in the Third World who would be glad of it.

Come to think of it plump, greedy Penny Gammon was watching Claire's leftovers with a wistful eye.

Don was in superb form and told a funny story of the time he had gone out to Hollywood in an attempt to break into the American film market. He'd arranged a lunch with a top agent but been fobbed off at the last minute with an underling called Marvin, who looked to be straight out of college.

He had, however, been impressed by the young man's command of his résumé and ability to get his name right. Until, halfway through lunch, Marvin had raised his hands, palms outward, to emphasise a point and Don had seen clearly written across his left palm in lurching black biro the words Andrew (Don) Donleavy and, on the right palm, *Space Pirates*. The agent had offered to take him on and Don had hardly been in a position to refuse, although he would have liked to. Nothing came of it, though, and two years later, he was politely dropped from the agent's list. Thank goodness. God forbid that we should ever have to go and live in LA.

Bill Gammon was a GP, although not our GP. I find the thought of being on social terms with my doctor vaguely obscene. Imagine sitting across the dinner table from someone who gave you a smear test the previous week. My doctor was Bill's junior partner, Ruth Springer. They were an old-fashioned set-up and I sometimes wondered if Bill kept up with the latest advances in medicine and, if not, whether he was any the worse a doctor for that.

He held out his glass now, stretching uninhibitedly past Claire Cross for a refill. "Come on, Don. Don't hog the good booze for yourself."

"I bought a case of it," Don said, laughing, "when Jen told me she'd invited you, Bill."

"Good stuff," he said. "'S'all right. Penny's driving."

"Don't I always?" his wife replied.

Don opened another bottle, the cork easing out with a satisfying slurping noise. "None of your plastic corks," he remarked, sniffing it, and Tim treated us to a brief lecture on why plastic corks were better than cork corks.

"Excellent grub, Jennifer," Bill said, turning to me. "The venison is superb. My old father was a butcher and he always said that it's the fat that gives meat its flavour."

"Bill wanted to be a surgeon at one time," his wife interrupted, "carry on the family tradition."

"You don't want to believe this rubbish they tell you nowadays about not eating fat and not drinking alcohol." He patted Suza's hand. "A little of what you fancy does you good."

"Hear, hear," she said, not attempting to remove her hand as I would have done.

The Crosses looked vaguely scandalised and I saw them living on a diet of muesli and skimmed milk. "Surely the evidence is incontrovertible," Claire said in that ultra-polite way that says, 'I think you're talking bollocks'.

"This year's evidence," Bill agreed. "When I was at medical school, people were told to drink a pint of milk a day – full fat, of course, since that was the only sort we had in those days. School kids were given it free at play time till Thatcher came and *snatched* it away from them."

He mimed a mad old woman wrenching a bottle out of milk out of a child's hand.

"Actually," Tim said stiffly, "we both voted for *Lady* Thatcher in the eighties and we're not afraid to say so."

"Now there's a surprise," Suza whispered to me.

Bill shifted slightly in his seat to get a better view of Claire. "You're much too thin, young lady. I've been watching you and you've hardly eaten a thing. Men like something they can get hold of in a woman, you know."

I almost choked on my red cabbage. Claire went red. Penny said mildly, "That will do, Bill," and Suza grinned at me in glee.

"Do tell us about your new book, Suza." Penny, despite her rough country manners, was sensitive to the embarrassment of others. I looked at her gratefully as she added, "Or do you hate to talk about work in progress?"

"I never do that," Suza said, "in case it vanishes into the ether. But I've got a new hardback out in a couple of weeks so I don't mind talking about that since it's a fait accompli, as you might say."

She and Penny talked across the table in this way for a few minutes while I served pudding. Penny was well read and they discussed the Booker shortlist. They agreed about some writers and not about others, but without acrimony.

I sat back and let them get on with it while Don charmed Claire Cross to make it clear that he didn't think she was too thin, and eventually got her smiling again. I caught his eye the length of the table and he raised his glass to me in tribute.

Penny helped me clear the pudding and stood around while I made coffee and noisy general conversation flowed through the door. The dogs raised their noses, excited by a visitor, but they were forbidden to leave their baskets on pain of my extreme displeasure. "I won't offer to start the washing up," Penny said, "since cosy old women like me are expected to do that."

"I certainly don't expect you to."

"Nor shall I apologise for Bill. I gave up doing that years ago and, anyway, I'm not his keeper."

"He only said what he thought." Her face *was* a bit like a pig's, I noticed, with its flat nose, small eyes and unpainted pinkness; but then I'd always had a soft spot for pigs.

"I like your Ms Darc," Penny was saying.

"Yes."

"I've been wanting to meet her. Interesting woman."

"Yes, she is." I lowered my voice and glanced back into the dining room. "I couldn't believe the nosy questions Tim was asking her, could you? So rude."

Penny replied, "When I was young it was rude to ask a woman her age. Now it's rude to ask her how much money she earns. Still, I can't imagine Suza gave him truthful answers."

I was shocked. "You mean she lied?"

"Why not, if people ask impertinent and intrusive questions they can expect to be lied to. I'm having a good time," she went on, opening cupboard doors at random to inspect the contents. "I like a lively debate. Most dinners we get asked to, people sit around telling you how much they paid for their house, how much it was worth at the peak of the market in 1988 and how dramatically it has fallen in value since. Either that or it's a bunch of bloody doctors putting you off your food with their disgusting symptoms. Unspeakably dull." She pulled open the fridge.

"You still hungry, Penny?" I asked rather snidely.

"No, love. Just snooping. Seaweed-flavoured pasta indeed! Where do you find these things?"

"Didn't you like it?"

"Oh, yes," she said. "I liked it." She shut the fridge and looked at me. "You do look lovely tonight, Jennifer. Have you lost weight?"

"No," I said, "hidden it under a designer dress."

"And you've done something to your hair. Very nice. There isn't any trouble, is there, dear?"

I was startled. "What on earth do you mean, Penny?"

"I have this stupid idea that when a woman who's been married a long time suddenly starts making a big effort with her appearance, it must mean that she suspects . . . that her husband is . . ." Seeing my face she came to an abrupt halt. "I'm a stupid and tactless old woman and you mustn't take any notice of me whatsoever."

I gave her a hug. "Really, Penny. It's nothing like that. You couldn't be wider of the mark."

"Oh," she said. "That's good." I handed her a tray of coffee cups to take through and she went obediently off. She paused in the doorway and said, "Alternatively, of course, it can mean that the woman herself has got her eye on another . . . on someone else."

"Oh . . . get that coffee in to them while it's hot!" I said, laughing at her absurdity.

# Grand slam

After dinner Don announced that he would like to play bridge. I objected that seven was hardly a suitable number and that he knew I was a duffer at cards. "Yes, Jen," he said kindly. "I do know. I noticed somewhere along the last quarter of a century that you're a duffer at cards."

The Gammons said they didn't play and Don began to look sulky and muttered that it was his birthday and that he hardly ever got a chance to play. I gave him a frosty look. He sounded like the spoilt child his widowed mother would have liked to make of him, and I hated couples who bickered in public.

It turned out that the Crosses were keen, however, and Suza agreed to make up a four, so then everyone was happy. It could have been worse, I suppose: he could have wanted us to play charades.

I took the Gammons to sit comfortably by the fire, while the bridgers disposed themselves about the quickly cleared table, Suza and Don being obliged to partner each other. Suza said cheerfully, "I haven't played for years, but I expect it'll soon come back to me." Don looked distinctly gloomy at this statement while the Crosses perked up no end. Tim suggested what he called a 'modest wager to give it some interest' and they settled on a penny a point.

Bill was staring again at Claire, whose blouse was distinctly see-through now we'd turned up the lights. "See what I mean?" he hissed. "Did she breastfeed? If so the kids must have half-starved. Oww!" Penny had kicked him, hard.

It rapidly became clear that Suza was a first-rate player and that her game suited Don's as a cork fits its bottle. On the third hand they bid and made a no-trump grand slam, vulnerable, and I could see my husband, who was the declarer, visibly swelling with pride as he drew out the last four cards and triumphantly announced the score.

You see how I know the jargon: all those evenings spent adoringly watching Don play bridge before curtain-up in Eastbourne, his face keeping his cards a secret behind his mask of Leichner, a Senior Service at a jaunty angle in his mouth.

Claire Cross glared at Suza who smiled serenely and said, "I said I hadn't played for years; I didn't say I wasn't any good. I played for my college." They went on in this way, with Don and Suza intermittently calling out things like, "Oh well played, partner!" and, "You two aren't having much luck tonight, are you?" The Crosses began to live up to their name, Claire nibbling the end of her pencil angrily as she jotted down the score.

Suza shuffled the cards the way people do in casinos on TV: so fast that they become a blur. Watching out of one eye, while keeping up a conversation about a variety of subjects with the Gammons, I could see the Crosses thought they'd been brought here to be fleeced in some sort of scam.

"If I wanted to get rich beyond the dreams of avarice—" Bill was saying.

"Which of course you don't."

"I wouldn't waste time trying to find a cure for cancer. No, sir. Pill to make women thin."

Finally, we realised that it was nearly midnight and the Gammons got heavily up, saying Bill had Saturday morning surgery. The Crosses were also only too willing to call a halt and grudgingly paid up twenty pounds in cash which Don and Suza scooped up with glee as if it was the National Lottery jackpot on a rollover week.

The Gammons offered to drop Suza off at Madder Cottage, which offer she accepted. She turned to kiss me goodbye; then, to my surprise, Don also presented her with his cheek. They kissed, his hand rubbing down her back as if they were old friends, as he said, "We must get up a four regularly." Clearly the way to my husband's heart is through the ace of trumps.

"Mmm," Suza said, *sotto voce*, looking over her shoulder at the Crosses, who were already banging into Tim's BMW with the minimum of valedictions. "We may have to find some other opponents, though. Goodnight, Jen. Mmm! I shall taste your wonderful floating islands all week. Goodnight, Andy. Thanks for a lovely evening."

Whispered recriminations could be heard on the night air as Tim and Claire argued about which of them had promised to stay sober enough to drive home. "Don't forget to watch my episode of *Inspector Crane* on December the eighth," Don called after them, but they didn't bother to reply.

"I do wish you wouldn't bankrupt my guests," I said with mock severity when I'd closed the door. It had done Claire Cross good to be taken down a peg. "We shan't get invited back."

He laughed. "Serve them right. They were the ones who wanted to play for money. They thought *they* could sting *us* when Suza said she was rusty. I'm fairly sure they had a secret code, anyway."

"You mean he picks his nose and she leads a trump? Wouldn't that get complicated after a while?"

"I suppose it does sound a bit unlikely when you put it like that," he admitted, "but they wouldn't be the first married couple to try it." He stretched his arms and yawned. "I haven't had such a good evening for a long time. Thanks for organising it, darling. The food was wonderful, as always."

"I'm glad you're happy."

He pulled his tie off and slung it across the back of a dining chair, loosening the collar of his green shirt. I sat down again by the fire, wanting to enjoy a last few minutes of quiet after all that noise and chatter, to collect my thoughts. I was bone tired but I could see that Don was hyped up, excited, and I knew he wouldn't go immediately to sleep. I didn't go into the kitchen. I couldn't face the sight of those plates and dishes and knives and forks waiting to be washed and put away in the morning. For the first time I pondered whether my refusal to install a dishwasher was sheer martyrdom. I wondered whether to pour myself another brandy and decided against it. I felt pleasantly muzzy.

Don paced up and down the room for a minute, talking about the evening's entertainment, reliving some of his slams. I wasn't listening; he didn't expect me to. Then he came over to stand by me.

"You look so beautiful tonight." He ran his fingers through my hair and said in a thick voice, "My red-headed vixen." He picked up my hand and kissed it; then he pressed my palm to the front of his trousers so I could feel his arousal. I looked up at him and the wine was in his eyes. "Extwa pwesent?" he suggested.

"Yes," I said with a smile. "Why not?" I got up. "Let's go up."

"No." He pulled me down on the floor in front of the fire. "Here. We'll christen the new hearthrug."

I woke at three in the morning with a terrible pain on the right side of my abdomen, below the breastbone. At some stage we'd crawled our way up to bed from the fireside and Don was lying curled warm and naked up against me, so I didn't want to move for fear of waking him. Finally, though, I could bear it no more. I sat up, pressing my hand to the pain with a gasp of distress. I needn't have worried, Don rolled over onto his back without waking, his left arm falling clear over his side of the bed.

He murmured, "Three no trumps."

I sat in the total darkness of the country on a cloudy night, trying not to panic. Indigestion? I chided myself for the thought; my cooking was not indigestible. I got quietly up and made my way to the window. I subsided on the padded seat, clutching my chest. I pulled back the velvet curtain. The garden seemed still and empty although I knew that it was, in reality, a funfair of activity, of gang warfare: mice, rats, foxes, squirrels, disputing the territory we foolishly thought of as ours.

I tried to think of anything but the pain and, after a while, it began to fade. I realised I was cold since Don had stripped me naked in the drawing room and I wasn't even wearing a nightdress. I blushed at the memory of it. I went back to bed, pressed my cool lips to my husband's sleeping cheek and, by morning, I had all but forgotten about it and wondered if it had been a dream.

# Creativity

"I might write a novel," Don said one day the following week, after lunch. I gaped at him in disbelief. He'd never previously expressed any such desire. "Useful to have two strings to your bow," he added. "You heard what Suza was saying at dinner the other night about how much she gets paid. There are a few actors who've made a go of it: Antony Sher, Herbert Lom—"

"I don't believe *you*!" I exploded. "Do you imagine that it happens, just like that? That you bash a novel out in a few weeks and then get a Jeffery Archer style contract?"

"How difficult can it be?"

"I'll tell you how difficult it can be: it took Suza three years to find a publisher for her first novel, and then it took six years and another three novels before people were starting to notice her, before she got many reviews, before she could earn anything like a living at it."

"Sooner I get started the better, then. All my fans will buy a copy."

One thing I will say for my husband: you can't beat him

for optimism. He takes it for granted that he'll succeed at anything he wants to do. This confidence is good in some ways, but can result in a painful crashing down to earth when, for example, the part he's set his heart on goes to someone else.

He always picks himself up, though.

"What makes you think you've got any talent?" I asked.

"Only one way to find out." He got up and pulled on his mackintosh since it was raining. "I shall go and ask Suza for some tips, right now. Seize the bull by the horns." He flexed his fingers. "Dig the old typewriter out of the attic, there's a good girl." As I'd been planning to spend a quiet afternoon drinking coffee with Suza myself and putting the wrongs of the world to rights, I sank down on the kitchen chair, defeated, dazed.

I imagined that Suza would give him short shrift and that he'd be back with his tail between his legs in half an hour, but I was wrong. Clearly their relationship had improved on the long train journey and with their triumphant routing of the Crosses at a simple card game.

All right, I thought when he wasn't back after an hour, I will take him at his word. I got the trapdoor hook from under the spare bed and pulled down the ladder. It was months, if not years, since anyone had been up in the loft, and quantities of dust showered on me. I turned my head away, coughing. I tested the ladder and climbed carefully up it. The cold-water tank was festooned in cobwebs. Luckily the lid was a firm fit or we'd've been washing our teeth in infant spiders. I found the typewriter easily but it looked small and tinny. I knew that Suza used a word processor – a clean, sharp screen that made a faint buzzing noise all the time – on which shoals of words shimmied out in neat and even lines. Then she would sometimes exclaim impatiently, highlight rows and rows of prose and – magic – they disappeared even faster than they'd come.

She had a number of hi-tech things – computers, a modem, teletext – that seemed so out of place at Madder Cottage that I could almost hear the walls grumble. Don and I had never even bothered to buy a CD player, being content with our records and tapes. I scorned the thought of a microwave oven, which was surely for idle cooks.

I made my way back down the ladder one-armed and took the machine into the kitchen with me. At first I put it in the sink, intending to run a stream of tap water through it; then that didn't seem such a good idea so I wet some J-cloths and began to swab it down. After what seemed an age the worst of the dust had gone and I put it on the table, slid the back of a circular that had arrived in that morning's post into the carriage and began to tap out nonsense about lazy foxes and quick brown dogs, or quick foxes and lazy brown dogs.

I'd done a typing course the summer I left school. My parents were willing – bless them – to indulge my whim of going to drama school but wanted me to have 'something to fall back on'. I hadn't done it for twenty-five years or more. There was something soothing about the rhythmic tapping. There used to be a tune based on the noise of a typewriter; you sometimes heard it on TV documentaries. It signified busyness and purpose, the music of a useful life.

What a pity Suza had that infernal computer, I thought. Otherwise I could offer to type for her, be in on the ground floor of her creation. As it was, if I wasn't careful, Don would remember my rusty skills and I would be in on the basement of his output. She did have a typewriter, bigger than ours, a sit-up-and-beg job. I'd noticed it tucked away on a shelf, too high for me to reach; kept, presumably, for emergencies and power cuts. Maybe she'd let me do some proof-reading or something. I'm nothing if not painstaking.

The machine was in fair condition only. The capital J didn't work at all. Don's hero – for he would surely want a male protagonist – had better not be called John. Oh, the whole idea was ridiculous.

I took the typewriter into the spare bedroom, complete with its lazy dog foxes and hid it under the bed where Don would never look. I went back down and made a cup of tea.

The phone rang a few minutes later. It was my friend. She sounded bemused, which was the nearest she ever got to being surprised, taken aback, shocked or embarrassed by anything. "I've just sent your handsome husband home," she said, "or he would have stayed all night. He'll be with you in five minutes."

"I'm sorry, Suza. I hope he wasn't too much of a nuisance."

"Not at all. I merely fed him good wine and got him to tell me some of his theatrical anecdotes. He soon forgot why he'd come."

"I can promise you I did everything possible to discourage him. It's not as though he's likely to be any good at it—"

"I'd be more worried if I thought he *might* be any good at it," she said. "There's too much competition out there as it is."

I heard the gate creak. "Here he is."

"Blimey," she said. "He must have run all the way back."

Which seemed unlikely. We giggled like conspirators and hung up. I told him I couldn't find the typewriter, that I must have given it to Oxfam years ago and he said he was thinking of getting a computer anyway. "You could do the accounts on it, Jennifer," he said, to my horror. "Might even enable us to dispense with the accountant. That way it'd pay for itself in the first year."

How did people make up stories, anyway? Was Don good at it? If so, should that worry me? Suza told me once that it's the detail that makes the tale ring true. It can't be easy being married to a writer, knowing that they can invent a plausible tale out of mid-air whenever they feel like it, people it with convincing characters and give them life and speech.

# Detail

"So how's your friend in Hammersmith?" I asked. "And her poor mother? I forgot to ask."

"Mmm?" Suza looked at me over a pair of large round spectacles. She'd been reading the news headlines on Ceefax when I arrived and had forgotten to take them off. In them she looked bookish and clever. "Oh, not so good, I'm afraid."

"What's happened?"

"They've taken the old lady into a nursing home. I helped Agnes pack her stuff, get her settled. She's unable to speak and doubly incontinent but it seems there's no real prospect of her dying unless and until she has another stroke and, since they've put her on a special diet and are giving her pills for her high blood pressure, that event seems remote. I call it cruel."

"Yes," I said. "I see what you mean."

"So poor Agnes now has to make time every day to visit a mother who no longer recognises her, or be consumed with guilt if she doesn't. And when the old lady dies – months, even years from now

– she'll torture herself with remorse because she'll be glad."

"So you were wrong," I said. "The situation hasn't resolved itself. The old woman hasn't died or got better. She's in limbo."

"No," she agreed. "There has been no resolution."

That's the worst state, I find, to be left dangling. Even a bad outcome is preferable. Once you know and accept the worst, you can pick yourself up and start rebuilding. Like when we knew for sure that we couldn't have children. Under the shock and disbelief, there was something like relief that the years of disappointed hope were over at last. Yes, relief: like the soldier in the front line who shoots himself through the head with his own gun rather than live with the uncertainty one more day.

"I took her shopping," Suza was saying, "to get some stuff for her mother, a warm flannel dressing gown, some new slippers. It was a frightful nuisance since it turns out she's afraid of lifts and we had to trail round the department stores going up and down the escalators."

"They seem to arrange the stores specially," I said, "so you have to go round each floor to get up to the next one."

"Hoping you will impulse buy. You see Agnes's way of dealing with a lift phobia is never to get in a lift. Mine would be to ride up and down in one, all day if necessary, until I'd overcome my darkest fear."

"Facing up to it rather than giving in to it?"

"Exactly."

"But what if the lift broke down and you got trapped?"

"That," she said with a laugh, "would be unfortunate." Forcing you to accept that your darkest fear was not so irrational after all. "Also," my friend went on, "the nursing home costs more than four hundred pounds a week and there's a possibility that Agnes will have to sell the flat to meet those bills since it technically belongs to mother."

"She never married, never left home?"

"Briefly, to go to Cambridge. Then went back, for good. Elderly parents, immigrants from some Mittel-European country, never at home in England or with the English language, very Anita Brookner. Stifling. You know how it is."

To be a child, always, in your parents' home. Can that be healthy?

"Its not about money, though, is it?" I said. "It never is."

She looked at me curiously. "What a sheltered life you've led, Jennifer. *It* is always about money, I find."

I protested but she went on, "I have a friend who's in love with a married man and he with her, but he can't leave his wife to be with her because she owns half his business, on paper, even though she's never done a day's work in it in her life. To leave her would be to lose – perhaps even to destroy – the business he's spent twenty years building up, the work that he's given his life to, and no woman can ask that of a man."

"A woman's support of her husband isn't always so tangible as you seem to think," I said bravely, since this hit close to home. "Often it's a case of boosting his morale, of being there with a smile and a large G&T when he gets home, exhausted; of keeping him going when he wants to give up. Your friend's lover's wife has given twenty years of her life to him. And maybe your friend should have thought twice before she fell in love with a man who wasn't free to love her back."

"You think we can choose where we love? You're full of surprises today, Jenny."

"I think there's always a moment," I said, "near the beginning, when we can choose to walk away . . ."

I almost did it myself, when I knew I was falling in love with Don, since I didn't see how I could win him or how, having won him, I could possibly keep him. I wanted not so much to walk away as to run, very fast like when you sprint away from a wasp before it can sting you.

He was so handsome and charming, so amusing, and, like most young women, I could see only the faults in myself – the small breasts and thick thighs, the hair that wasn't blond and the nose that wasn't pert.

Summer rep is hectic: you're performing one play while rehearsing another and learning the lines for a third. But one afternoon the director was rehearsing only the two principals and both Don and I had some time off. I was genuinely astonished when he asked me, almost shyly, if I would take a walk along the coast with him towards Beachy Head. Half an hour later we were walking together along the sea front, heading west. On the promenade fifty or sixty elderly people were docilely listening while the band played 'Take a Pair of Sparkling Eyes'.

"We'll be like that in sixty years' time," I said, nodding my head at them. "Sitting on the sea front in crimplene cardigans listening to Gilbert and Sullivan."

"No, they'll play the best of the Rolling Stones for us," he said, "and we'll sit there gently twitching to 'I can't get no satisfaction'." He slid his arm round my shoulder. "Are you always this cheerful?"

We soon outwalked the tourists and made our way up onto the cliffs. We found a shelter and sat on the bench reading the graffiti. It was explicit but not imaginative. One piece made me go red. Don, seeing my discomfiture, took out his pen and deftly altered one of the words so that it read, *Marilyn Brown gives good headlines*, which made me laugh.

He must have found me a poor companion since I was as tongue-tied as any of those young girls who worship him at conventions, lurching out mostly monosyllabic replies to his questions and comments, but it didn't stop him seeing me home the next night and every night after that.

I'd thought I liked men who were blond and well built. Don was thin and dark and he was the most beautiful thing I'd ever seen.

We became lovers the following Sunday afternoon. He'd accompanied me to mass that morning and my last thought as he led me upstairs to his bedroom and slid the bolt across was that I wouldn't be able to take communion again for the foreseeable future, since I had no intention of repenting of what I was about to do.

He seemed unsurprised at my virginity, as if it was no more than his due. I waited until the last minute to tell him in case he found the thought of deflowering me too daunting. When I finally whispered my guilty secret in his ear he said simply, "I know."

He was gentle and patient and, when I apologised for my breasts, said, "Too small for whom? In comparison with what? They feel fine to me."

We had to be quiet in case his landlady heard us. House rule number one: *no dragging back.*

Obviously it wasn't *his* first time but I never asked about my predecessors. They didn't seem important.

A few weeks later, summer season was coming to an end. I was terrified he would say, "Bye, Jen. It's been fun. See you around." Finally I plucked up the courage to ask him what would happen in the autumn and he said, "I thought we'd go up to London."

"London?" The only word I heard was *We.*

"That's where the work is, where the agents and producers are, where the auditions are held. We'll find a cheap flat, somewhere like Earls Court or Notting Hill. It'll be a hovel but after that things can only get better." He leaned over and stubbed his cigarette out in the ashtray on my bedside table. ". . . What's the matter, Jenny, don't you want to come with me?"

"Of course I do, more than anything. It's just . . . my

parents will be so miserable if they think I'm living with a man, in *sin*."

He stroked my breasts. "And you mind what they think?"

"Yes, of course I do." I had a close and loving relationship with my parents and I couldn't face the thought either of hurting them or of lying to them.

He said, "What if we tell them we're getting married soon?"

I couldn't speak for a moment, then I said, or rather gulped, "Was that a proposal?"

"Of course." He began to laugh. "Sorry. I didn't do that right, did I? It should have been down on one knee. *Jennifer, I love you madly. Will you be my wife?* That sort of thing. Although I suspect that most proposals nowadays take place like this, post-coitally."

"It doesn't matter," I said.

"Well?"

"Yes!"

Not a single one of my aunts omitted to take my mother on one side to ask if I'd got myself knocked up, that I was in such a hurry. I deliberately chose a tight dress as I knew my waistline would be under lascivious scrutiny . . .

"Jenny?" Suza was waving her hand in front of my face. "Anybody home?"

"Yes," I said again, picking up the thread of my thought, "there is always a moment, however fleeting, when you can turn back."

"It's not that easy," she said. "They see each other every day."

"They work together?"

"Something like that."

# The power of the dog

It was the beginning of November and no more had been said about the 'novel', nor about the computer, thank goodness. I was always the first up since Don liked a cup of tea in bed. When I pulled the bedroom door open at half-past seven one cold, dark morning, Aggie was lying on the landing as usual, her back against the airing cupboard, her legs spread wide.

"Where's Scamper?" I asked, and she wagged her tail and jumped up to follow me down the stairs.

I prepared the dogs' breakfast and called once, twice, three times but there was no sign of the younger dog. I wasn't unduly worried. It wouldn't be the first time Scamper had managed to squeeze her small body out through the larder window, or the old cat flap we'd inherited from the previous owner and never bothered to block up, or some other unlikely egress. I would find her sitting on the front doorstep, cold, hungry and slightly shame-faced.

But the step was innocent of anything except two pints of semi-skimmed and a carton of orange juice. I shrugged, made the tea and took it upstairs, climbing back into bed to warm my feet.

"Don't do that!" he snapped, his warm thighs receding before my questing soles. At least it had woken him up.

"When did you last see Scamper?" I asked him.

He thought about it. "I took them both out for a pee last thing. Then I left them curled up in the kitchen."

"Only there's no sign of her."

He shrugged. "She'll turn up. She's one of nature's wanderer's, not like Aggie, who's one of nature's home lovers."

"Bit like you and me when you come to think about it," I said. "The wanderer and the home bird."

"And the wanderer comes back when he's tired and hungry." His hand slid up under my nightdress, parting my thighs. "Or whatever."

"Mmm."

There's not a great deal to do in the garden in November but there were a lot of newly fallen leaves to be raked up. I wondered if I should make a bonfire for Guy Fawkes' night. I had a childlike attitude towards fireworks: glee mingled with terror, the never-conquered fear that some irresponsible small boy, as it might be Don, would throw a banger into my hair.

I made a mental note to keep the dogs in that night, which reminded me that there was still no sign of Scamper. If she wasn't home by lunchtime I would set off to the village in search of her.

Aggie came out to join me: she liked to play in the piles of leaves and I pretended to chase her away with my rake. She got excited and began to bark, running in wider and wider circles over the quarter-acre of wild terrain which passes for our back garden.

I noticed immediately the change in tone as she stopped running abruptly and began to bay, her feet four-square in the long grass behind the compost heap, her head thrown back: the picture of a dog in distress. I dropped my rake and ran towards her: it could be anything – a nest of rats, even an adder, dangerously disturbed at the start of her hibernation.

I wished I'd kept hold of the rake.

I saw the body of Scamper, or what remained of it, as soon as I rounded the compost. I'd once seen the hunt pass through my village as a child, seen a neighbour's cat torn into pieces by the hysterical hounds, heard its screams as it died, the neighbour's anguished disbelief.

A thirty-five-year-old nightmare come back to haunt me. I turned my head away, wanting to vomit. Stumbling, I ran back up the garden calling for my husband, sobbing in pain.

"A fox," Don said. He looked grown up, his face sombre. His green and purple waterproof was wrong, too jolly. "Poor little bugger," he said.

"How could a fox do *that*?" I pointed a trembling finger. Scamper's throat had been bitten through, her head hanging grotesquely loose, her floppy ears soaked with blood. Her belly had been half ripped open. There was a great deal of blood too on the damp grass which suggested that she hadn't died quickly.

"A big old dog fox in search of food," he said, "looking for our dustbins. Scamper was in the wrong place at the wrong time."

If only it had been Aggie, I found myself thinking. She was an old lady, not long for this world anyway; Scamper was a baby with her life before her. "Pity it wasn't Aggie," Don said. "She'd have stood some chance, big fat thing like her."

The quick brown fox tears open the little dog.

"Isn't there anything we can do?" I'd never felt so helpless.

"What? Call the police? Report a murder? Charge Brer Fox and have him hanged?"

"Stop it! I can't bear it!" I found myself beating at his chest with my fists. "I can't bear this *flippancy* at a time like this."

I began to sob and he took me tightly in his arms, anchoring my flailing fists against my sides, smoothing my hair. "I'm sorry, baby. It's my way of coping. There isn't anything we can do. Nature is red in tooth and claw."

"I'm not having another," I sobbed. "I can't bear it. Do you hear me?"

"Shh, shh. We shall see. You said you wouldn't have another when Martha died."

"I mean it. I mean it."

He sat me down on the bench, fetched a spade from the shed and dug a deep hole under the apple tree next to where Martha was buried. He gathered up the remains of Scamper from the mess of footprints and put her in a Sainsbury's carrier bag and dropped it into the hole. He put the earth back and made a tight mound. Two thin apple twigs were lashed together with string to make a cross.

Aggie lay down in front of the grave, her head on her paws and keened.

Don made me go back indoors in the warm. Aggie stayed and mourned her companion until dusk fell.

The first thing Don did was to call Suza. I heard him speaking quietly into the telephone, glancing at me once or twice as I sat numbly at the kitchen table. Then he poured me a glass of brandy and said, "Suza will be right up. She'll know what to do."

She drove up as it was an emergency and appeared within five minutes, coming in at the kitchen door without knocking. She didn't say a single word but took me in her arms and hugged me. I could feel the fast pulse of her neck against mine. Her breathing was harsh, the way it was when she was suffering an asthma attack. "Excuse me," she said after a moment, releasing me. She took a blue inhaler from her pocket and breathed it in. Then again. I felt a sense of anticlimax.

"Are you okay?" I asked.

"Bugger it!" she said. "I'm the one who's supposed to ask you that."

It hurt too much to smile but she made coffee for us, my neat kitchen being now as familiar to her as her own untidy den. I noticed that Don had taken the opportunity to leave the room and I could dimly hear him in the study on the phone, no doubt to his agent. I added another tot of brandy to my coffee and began to feel more human, a little less as if I might go mad. She was wheezing slightly. "Is it the damp?" I asked.

"Possibly. But more likely it was Leo Apter's horse. You know how I am with anything furry."

"Horses are hardly furry."

She shrugged. "Same difference. Same allergy. She caught me at the front gate this morning as I was slipping back from the village shop with a pint of milk. I was stuck out there for a good ten minutes, without a coat, while the bloody animal calmly ate my hedge!"

"I like Leo," I said, irrelevantly.

"Oh, she's all right. Bit of a cold fish." I remembered that Leo had once been the nearest thing I had to a friend round here. I wondered if she was feeling neglected since Suza's arrival. "I don't like horses," Suza said. "They're so damn big! And they stand there, munching, looking at you as if they know something you don't – presumably what my hedge tastes like."

I tried to smile but started to cry instead.

"Oh, Jenny." She took my hand across the table and began to recite. "'There is sorrow enough to the natural way from men and women to fill our day; but when we are certain of sorrow in store, why do we always arrange for more? Brothers and sisters, I bid you beware, Of giving your heart to a dog to tear.'"

I found the rumpty-tumpty rhythm soothing, like a drumbeat. I wiped my eyes on my free wrist and sniffled. "I don't know it."

"Kipling: 'The Power of the Dog'."

"It was something to love," I said.

She looked at me oddly, and perhaps it was a strange thing for a happily married woman to say.

The doorbell rang that afternoon. It was Leo Apter. Without her horse. "I came to say how sorry I was to hear about the puppy," she said.

"Who told you?" I snapped.

She looked surprised that I should need to ask. "Mrs Price." Who else? She held out a small paper parcel. "I was baking and I thought you might like this for your tea; it's chocolate; your favourite."

Which reminded me that I'd often gone to Stratford House for tea, in another life. Just as I'd sometimes gone riding with her, in another life. I took the cake. Comfort eating: there's no logic in it but the fact is that it works. I even went out and gave Aggie some choc drops after lunch as if she shared this human idiocy.

"You'd better come in," I said.

Perhaps my reluctance made itself heard in my voice since she backed away from the doorstep, her hands making a deprecatory motion. "I won't disturb you, Jenny.

I wanted you to know that I was thinking of you." Which made me feel like a heel.

Aggie wouldn't leave my side after Scamper's death if she could help it. If I got up to go to the lavatory she would immediately jump up and follow me, sitting patiently outside the door until I'd finished. If I threw a stick for her on our walks she would lumber after it, right enough, but with frequent turns of her golden head to ensure that I hadn't taken the opportunity to run away and die. If I went out in the car she would be in a state of acute distress on my return.

"She'll soon forget," Don said kindly, but how could he know?

# Blooper

I walked down to Madder Cottage at lunchtime one Friday morning in mid-November. Suza had been away for a few days teaching a creative writing course somewhere in the North, and had returned only the previous evening. I didn't bother to knock but went round to the back door and pushed it open as usual. I found her squinting at a *Space Pirates* video, or rather at the box.

"Hello!" I said, surprised. "Been converted to fandom?"

"Andy dropped a couple round last night," she said. "Said I might find them amusing."

"Did he?" He hadn't mentioned it. He'd taken Aggie for her late walk at about nine o'clock and had been out longer than usual. I'd assumed, without bothering to ask, that he'd dropped into the Old Piper for a quick one.

"I watched a bit before I went to bed," she said. "He's right: it *is* amusing. Beats *Newsnight* any day. I especially liked the bit where he swings down on a rope and almost falls over when he lands."

I laughed. "That's one of my favourite bits too."

"I'd always assumed – call me Queen Naive of the Naive People – that bloopers like that were reshot."

"They are normally, but by halfway through the first series of *Pirates* they were so far behind schedule that they were only just getting the episodes edited in time for transmission and there was no leeway for any fancy retakes merely because somebody had fluffed their lines or fallen over the furniture. It was a nightmare."

"It's not actually sci-fi at all," she mused. "It's an old-time pirate story that happens to be set in outer space. Sci-fi is a real leap of the imagination – *1984*, *Brave New World*, *The Handmaid's Tale*. It's not a genre I've ever assayed but think of the freedom, the complete liberty of the imagination to roam." She looked deflated. "Too much freedom, perhaps. Is that why it's seldom successful?"

I poured myself a mug of coffee from the filter and sat down at the table. It had been such a long time ago but I could remember Don coming home exhausted and dissatisfied and swearing he would never sign up for a second series of *Pirates*, in the unlikely event of there being one. He had, of course, when they offered him enough money.

She was staring at the box. "I'm trying to make these pictures out," she explained. The video boxes had photos from the series on the back, but the fronts were an odd representational – cartoon-like – mess. "I mean," she went on, "this is presumably meant to be Andy here, but his face is squashed up and a peculiar colour, like he was an alien." She snapped her fingers. "That's it! It's a post-modernist concept: Captain Will Davenant *is* an alien to the aliens he meets, beats up, robs and kills."

"I think they just had a crap artist," I said, giggling.

"You can be prosaic, Jennifer," she said. "It's so much more satisfying to search for the least likely explanation." She lost interest in the video, dropping it on the table in a pile of scrap paper and said, "Lunch!"

"Don was good-looking in those days," I said wistfully.

"He still is!"

I noticed that she was looking smart today. She'd had her hair cut to the point where it curled onto her shoulder, looking glossy and healthy. She was wearing a light foundation and, surely, some lipstick on her full lips. She had also – most unusually – put on a skirt, and I saw that she had good legs, shapely, not too thin and bony, elegant ankles, no ladders in her tights. I remembered again that she'd struck me, at first meeting, as a handsome woman.

Don claims that he prefers women to girls, that the skinny, blond twenty-five-year-olds he sometimes has to act with have no intelligent conversation, no character, no *history*.

This may be to put me off the scent.

She put slices of white bread in the toaster and stuck a tin of baked beans in the electric can-opener, decanting them into a jug for the microwave. No man was ever going to want Suza for her culinary skills.

"I saw the hunt out the other day," she mused. "Much

as one feels one should deplore it as savage and outdated, it is quite a spectacle. Makes me wish I was a painter – those equine muscles and men with faces as red as their coats. It seems like an aesthetic crime to ban it."

"Did the hunt kill?" I asked casually.

"Dunno."

I was thinking they might have got the quick brown fox that killed Scamper. If so, I hoped it hadn't been a fast or painless death.

It might have been a nightmare when I saw Mrs Jensen's cat torn apart by the hunt when I was eleven, but it was exhilarating too.

Call me savage and outdated.

# Reflections

When I came out of the bathroom the next morning, Don was standing naked in front of the full-length mirror on the bedroom wall. As I stood in the doorway, silently watching him, he turned this way and that, sucking in his stomach, throwing out his chest. He looked comic: a pallid, middle-aged man with heavy thighs and a small pot belly, his private parts bulging redly beneath it. The small patch of fuzz on his chest was mostly grey and there were some streaks of white in his pubic hair.

He had a high colour, I noticed, his cheeks flushed beneath his morning stubble. "I could do with losing a few pounds," he said, surprising me since I'd thought he didn't know I was there. "Toning up a bit. Don't you think?"

He didn't turn round and I realised that he could see me perfectly well in the looking-glass and was addressing himself to my reflection, to another, more nebulous Jennifer. "I like you the way you are," I replied. "I don't mind a few extra pounds. Why would I?"

"Wrong answer, Jennifer. What you should have said

is, 'You have the same slender, boyish figure you had twenty-five years ago'."

"Love is blind, but not *that* blind." I put my arms round his waist, resting my chin on his shoulder. "Your body is beautiful," I said, "designed by nature for the delight of women." He duly laughed but he didn't put butter on his toast that breakfast, dipping dry soldiers into his boiled egg.

We always had wine with dinner and he usually had a Scotch or two after it, but not that evening. As I served supper I had the vague sense that something was missing from the table and then I realised what it was: a green bottle, opened a couple of hours earlier, that it might breathe. I made no comment but he said, "Thought I'd give the old liver a rest for once."

"Good idea."

"Anyway, alcohol is empty calories, you know."

"I know," I said. "I'm surprised that you do." The number of men who tell you they need a bottle of red wine a day to stave off anaemia, as though this was a serious menace.

"Oh, I was having a look at the diet of the week in your magazine. It seems straightforward enough. Basically one eats less!"

I raised my eyebrows but said nothing; my intermittent attempts at dieting were met with derision or impatience and were soon abandoned in the teeth of opposition, of demands to know when we would have 'proper food' again.

I took my place at the table and passed him the serving spoon, lifting the lid of the dishes to allow savoury steam to assault our senses. It was chicken casserole in cider with baby carrots, broccoli and mashed potatoes; he took a small portion of each, half what he would usually have as a first helping. The green and orange and white collage – like the flag of Éire – looked insignificant on his big white plate.

I felt annoyed. He might have warned me that half my lovingly prepared stew would be wasted. Aggie would feast tonight.

I didn't expect this new puritanism to last.

I was wrong. Two weeks later he'd lost half a stone and his beer belly was noticeably less prominent. He'd joined a gym ten miles away on the outskirts of Ipswich and drove over two or even three mornings a week, coming home two hours later, glowing with health, his hair damp from the shower. He would insist on doing a dozen sit-ups before coming to bed. Like all recent converts he was becoming a bore on the subject of diet and fitness and I saw Suza stifle a yawn on more than one occasion.

"Has he had his midlife crisis?" she asked me.

"Certainly not!"

"Well he's having it now, then. Bit late, but there we are. I had mine when I was thirty-two, which is, perhaps, premature."

"What happened?" I asked.

She waved the question away. "It isn't interesting. It

never is. If only someone would invent a new type of midlife crisis for people to have, one in which they make *sensible* changes in their lives instead of destroying everything that's gone before. You watch: he'll be dying his grey hair and buying expensive new aftershave. You'd better keep an eye on him."

I said drily, "I always do."

It's a cruel admission but I tried to sabotage him. Everyone agrees that I'm a terrific cook and I brought forth my best recipes, and put extra cream and butter in them. I made his favourite puddings – oozing crumbles of late-autumn fruits, plums, pears, laden with sugar and served with home-made custard; double chocolate terrine with cream. I made fools.

He didn't refuse anything, thus allowing me a full-scale row, but would eat a little of each, praise it to the skies, and refuse seconds.

His will-power was infuriating. He'd given up drinking completely until he reached his target of twenty pounds lost. One night I opened a bottle of his favourite Hérmitage and wafted the rich aromatic bouquet under his nose, but he wasn't tempted. I drank it myself and my head throbbed alarmingly in the morning. He was disappearing before my eyes. It was frightening. Where were the missing pounds of him going?

He looked younger, even more handsome. He was dashing Will Davenant again. His cheeks were less ruddy. The instructor at the gym apparently praised his declining blood pressure. He walked taller. One day he said, "I wish I'd done this years ago."

He made me feel inadequate. Not only did he put in perspective my pathetic attempts to lose weight over the years, but I felt I'd lost my purpose in life. The way to a man's heart was supposed to be through his stomach and I'd followed this well-trodden route of cordon bleu love from our earliest days. Now I might as well serve up ready-made lasagne from Sainsbury's as other wives did, as Penny Gammon did.

"It'll help my career," he said. "I can be a hero again, the love interest, not just a tooth-gnashing baddie."

He got some new publicity photos done.

# Well-wisher

One evening we were sitting watching a bad old film – melodrama, circa 1975 – in which Don makes a two-minute appearance as a young hospital doctor and says, 'We shall have to have you in to do some more tests next week, Mrs Miller.'

Although we were amused by the costumes and hair-styles – the Rod Stewart-style layer cuts and twenty-inch flares – it was a tense experience. The film was on ITV and there was a danger they would have edited out Don's scene to make room for an extra Persil advert, in which case we would be going disgruntled to bed. Fortunately, that didn't happen this time. After we'd giggled at Don's shoulder-length curls framing his smooth boy's face, the face of a stranger, we didn't bother to watch any more of the film but went upstairs.

I suppose in this democratic age of the video it will become normal for people to have their every experience recorded, to be able to replay a lifetime's memories, see those earnest young strangers whose sensations are long forgotten, unrecapturable even by the imagination.

For some reason we slept late. I awoke in time to hear the plopping of the morning post through the letterbox, as delivered by Postman Stan in his little red van. I yawned, slid out of bed, pulled my quilted dressing gown on, groped under the bed for my slippers and went downstairs.

"Bill, bill," I muttered under my breath, shuffling the envelopes, "circular, *Casting News*."

The last envelope was a nondescript white one, good quality, the size that takes a sheet of A4 paper folded twice. It was addressed, by rackety typewriter, to 'Mrs A. P. Donleavy', which seemed old-fashioned and pre-feminist. The address was precise and full – The White House, Stratford End, Nr Stratford St James – and the post code. Intrigued, I slit it open with my finger, took out the one sheet of white A4 it contained and unfolded.

There was no heading and no salutation and the type-written message was only three lines long, four if you counted the signature, such as it was.

> Are you blind? Can't you see what's going on
> on your own doorstep? Take better care of him,
> or lose him.
>
> A well-wisher

I examined at the envelope. It was postmarked Ipswich the previous afternoon. I felt cold. Whoever had sent this message was close by, perhaps very close. I'd been in Ipswich myself at that time, had perhaps passed my enemy as she – for it was surely a she; were not anonymous letters always from a she? – had slipped this piece of poison into the pillar box. The reasonableness of the tone, the clarity, the lack of needless elaboration, only made it more chilling.

Better take care of him: it echoed, strangely, Suza's words – *You'd better keep an eye on him.*

"Anything for me?" Don called down the stairs.

With an unshaking voice, I replied, "Just some bills."

"Any chance of a cup of tea?"

"Coming right up."

I put the kettle on; while it boiled, I took paper and envelope into the drawing room and burned them on the ashes of yesterday's fire.

As I went back into the kitchen, I felt that pain again, the one I'd had after the dinner party, the one I convinced myself I'd imagined. I reeled to the sink and vomited nothingness, a few retches of green bile from a stomach emptied by the night.

I clutched my chest, sank down on the kitchen chair, laid my head on the table and wept silently until the kettle boiled.

# Ulceration

When I mentioned my pains to Don I saw his face close up with irritation. He hates illness. He's not even registered with a GP himself. He could be a Christian Scientist, so strongly does he disbelieve in sickness. According to him there is nothing that can't be cured by a whisky and hot lemon and the lemon is optional.

"I'm sure it's nothing," he said brusquely. "Spot of indigestion."

For once I stood up for myself. "We're getting to that age now when we can't afford to take a cavalier attitude to our health any more, Don. It could be heart disease. It could be cancer."

"Nonsense. You know that I rely on you to outlive me, Jenny. How can you be so selfish?"

"It could be an ulcer."

"Ah." It seemed he was prepared to compromise on an ulcer. "Well, that's not too serious, is it? A bland diet for a few weeks, isn't that the treatment?"

"Fine!" I said. "Then we shall live on beans on toast for the next six weeks."

He grinned. "Let's not be hasty, Jen. If I wanted to live on beans on toast, I'd've stayed a bachelor. Or married Suza."

Suza was no more encouraging.

"I haven't much faith in doctors," she explained. "I had a friend, a poet, up in London a few years ago, started having difficulty swallowing. Finally went to the doctor who diagnosed stress and prescribed Valium. In fact he had cancer."

She stopped and it seemed that was the end of the story. "What happened?" I asked.

"Oh, he died."

"Well, thanks for the reassurance!"

"Did his career no end of good," she said.

The next morning I came back from the shops to find Don in his favourite armchair, engrossed in Suza's latest hardback. "Suza dropped this in while you were out," he said. "She didn't stop."

He was about twenty pages into it. I took the top of the book between thumb and forefinger and tweaked it out of his grasp.

"Hey!" he said.

"Mine, I think."

"I was reading that."

"She's *my* friend," I hissed. "She brought the book for *me*."

He folded his arms. "Oh, don't be so childish, Jen.

Anyway, that wasn't what she said. She said, 'I thought I'd drop a copy of my new book in for you.' *You*: that means both of us. Or else it meant *me*, since I was the only one here."

"You can borrow it when I've finished with it." I dropped it in my bag. "And now I'm going to see the doctor. I may be some time."

"See you later, Captain Oates."

# Holistic medicine

I went to the doctor's house to ask if Dr Springer could possibly fit me in that morning, but the receptionist told me that she had gone on holiday for two weeks. "Thailand," she enthused. "Isn't that lucky?" Not for me.

She offered me a locum whom I didn't know. So I agreed to see Bill Gammon, who could squeeze me in, it seemed, after his last appointment. I took a seat. This was not a purpose-built health centre, modern and antiseptic. It was an Edwardian semi on the outskirts of Woodbridge. The waiting room was the front sitting room and Bill's surgery must once have been the dining room.

I'd never found out what went on upstairs although Penny insisted it was a brothel.

There were health posters on the wall but they were old and torn. Not one of them was about Aids. There were ashtrays instead of no-smoking signs and that made me smile as being so typically Bill.

I knew that his surgery always ran late. Instead of giving each patient a punctilious eight minutes, or whatever it was, Bill would sit and chat, often for half an hour, until he was certain he'd got to the root of the problem, that a recurring pain wasn't a wounded heart, a teenage daughter who might be pregnant or on drugs, an unfaithful husband, a lost job.

I was glad that I'd brought Suza's new book. I took it out of my bag and studied the dust jacket at my leisure. A recent photo of my friend took up half the back: she looked glamorous, relaxed, happy, successful. On her face was the half smile I knew so well. Suza laughed a lot but she wouldn't smile to order. It was an imposition, she said, demanded of women by society, that they ingratiate.

Beneath the photo were paeans of praise for her previous novels from people like Malcolm Bradbury and Rose Tremain.

I didn't read the blurb on the inside front cover. I preferred to find out for myself what the story was about, not have it spoilt for me in advance. Turning the pages, I saw that Suza had crossed through her printed name on the title page and replaced it with her signature and an inscription: *Dearest Jennifer, with all my love, Suza*, and the date.

There, I knew the book was only for me.

I'd read six chapters by the time I was called in to see Bill. Suza's books were set in London and I wondered if her translation to the country would mean a change of fictional scene too. I found most of her characters hard to like – uncaring husbands, unloved wives, unscrupulous mistresses – but fascinating. I wondered if her bad experience of marriage had soured her irrevocably for loving relationships, or whether all she needed was a period of healing.

I hoped so: I wanted my friend to be happy, to find a man of her own to love.

Bill had to ring for me twice. I was the only person left in the waiting room by then. I rushed into his consulting room finally, a little flustered and apologising.

"Gone to sleep out there?" he asked with a chuckle. "Don't blame you. Nothing so boring as waiting to see the quack."

"No," I said. "On the contrary. I was engrossed in what I was reading."

"So what can I do for you?"

I explained. He didn't offer to examine me but stared out of the window for a moment. Then he leafed through my notes. "There's all this talk now about holistic medicine," he said, "about treating the whole person and not the individual symptoms, as if that wasn't what any halfway decent doctor has been doing since Hippocrates lanced his first boil."

He read out my date of birth. "May 23rd 1949? That makes you . . . thirty-eight? That can't be right."

"*Forty*-eight."

"Of course." He smiled at me out of his kind, crumpled face. "Arithmetic was never my strong point. Started the change yet, Jenny?"

"No."

"Nothing?"

"Still as regular as clockwork."

"Well, that's something to look forward to – huge hormonal surges and irrational anger, ramming your shopping trolley into innocent ankles. Ask Penny."

"I can't wait."

"Worried about anything?" I shook my head. "Not feeling a bit depressed lately?"

"I don't think so. Can one tell?"

"You mean if you're really depressed, you're probably too depressed to notice?"

"Something like that."

"Interesting point. What about your puppy? Penny told me about that. It must have been a blow. Fox, wasn't it? Nasty, aggressive, disease-ridden brutes. Townies think they're cute, you know, red and bushy. Brer Fox."

"Oh yes, it was a blow at the time. But it's not as if she was the first I've lost. When you keep pets, you have to reconcile yourself to the idea that their lifespan is strictly limited." Grief, so poignant, so seemingly perpetual, had faded, as it does, and I could no longer remember what it felt like. "I suppose I've always considered myself a pretty happy and lucky person, Bill: lovely husband, nice home, no money worries; that sort of thing."

"Quite right," Bill said. "I'm not even sure I believe in depression. Half the time when people come to me saying, 'Oh, Doctor Gammon, I'm so depressed,' it turns out that what they are is *unhappy* and even the most competent pharmaceutical company – if that isn't a contradiction in terms – hasn't come up with a cure for that yet. Comes on mostly at night, you say?"

"Yes. I wake up in the small hours with this awful pain below my ribs." I pointed to the place. "Although, once, it happened when I was making early-morning tea."

I faltered but Bill didn't seem to notice. Worried? What about that anonymous letter. Why didn't I tell him about it? Because I liked to be seen as happy, successful, lucky – not as the sort of woman who received cruel notes about her husband from someone too embarrassed to sign her name.

"Been sick?" he asked.

"Once."

"And did that make the pain stop?"

"Yes," I said, having thought about it, "for a while."

Bill stroked his chin where he used to have a small beard until Penny said she couldn't stand it any more because there were always leftovers in it. "Sounds like a duodenal ulcer, which is partly why I asked if you'd been worrying lately – under stress, as we must say now."

"I'd have said I lead a pretty stress-free life," I said with a laugh, "walking, shopping, drinking coffee with my friend, a little light housework . . . and pots of gardening, of course."

What could be healthier?

"I'm not altogether convinced that stress is caused by change," Bill said. "That's too pat for my taste. Sometimes people *need* change, a bit of stimulation."

He'd taken me by surprise. "You think I'm bored?"

What was it you kept hearing people say these days? *Get a life.* So rude.

"An intelligent woman like yourself, no children to fuss over. It's easy to get introverted." Was he going to tell me to get a job too, I wondered? Was this some sort of conspiracy? I looked at Bill and saw old Mr Gammon, the butcher, with his boning knife.

"Still," he went on, "ulcers are easily dealt with these days." He picked up his prescription pad. "I shall prescribe some pills and you might think about sticking to a fairly bland diet for a while. Eat little and often to make sure your stomach is never completely empty. Go easy on the booze. Keep some dry biscuits by the bed for night pains."

He tore the prescription off and handed it to me. "Twice a day before meals. Come and see me again in a fortnight and we'll see how you're going on. Have you as right as rain in a month, you'll see."

"Are there any side effects I should watch out for?"

He made a tutting noise. "Don't ask me to put ideas into your head, a suggestible woman like you. If I tell you it might turn your toes green, you'll do nothing but watch your feet for the next two weeks." He got up and reached for his shabby jacket. "Actually, without prejudice to that – as my son-in-law, the lawyer, would say – don't drive if you get blurred vision or feel in any way confused. Couple of house calls to make. I saw Don the other day, out walking the dog late near Madder Cottage. He was looking awfully well, I must say."

"He's been on a diet," I said, "lost a stone and a half, getting himself fit, given up smoking."

Bill laughed. "He'll be taking up jogging next!"

I got the prescription made up. I went home and made myself a bland cheese sandwich and ate it with a glass of milk. I settled down to a quiet afternoon with my new book.

> *'It's a well-documented phenomenon,' said Deirdre with a wry smile. 'When a man wants to dump his wife, he tarts her up first to improve her chances of finding another man to support her.'*
>
> *'Quite right,' laughed Julian. 'Who was it said that paying alimony to an ex-wife is like buying carrots for a dead donkey?'*

I put the book, face down, on the arm of my chair and stared into nothingness. I knew what Suza said – that the opinions of her characters were not necessarily her own views – but something must have put that idea into her head in the first place.

Was my friend trying to warn me?

Was that what was happening to me?

Was I being fattened up for the slaughter?

I got another letter the following Wednesday, also post-marked Ipswich on Tuesday afternoon, market day. It's not worth recording the exact words, then or later. All through that autumn, they scarcely varied. *Are you blind? Are you mad? Are you pathetic? Sorry the man who shits on his own doorstep.*

Confident the man who shits on his own doorstep.

# Bitch

Our bedroom is at the back and, although the house is old and predates the age of noise pollution, the walls are thick and impervious to sound. So I was oblivious to anything out of the ordinary until the doorbell shrilled at seven one morning. Don grunted and pretended not to wake up. I put my dressing gown on and ran down the stairs as the bell went again, horribly insistent.

"All right! All right! I'm coming."

I wrenched the door open and found the milkman standing on the step holding a couple of bottles in his hands. His float stood beyond the picket fence, half blocking the lane. "Surely I paid you last week," I snapped, angry at being dragged so peremptorily from my bed.

"I saw the damage," he said, "and I was worried, like, in case anything had happened. You hear such stories nowadays about people being attacked in their own homes and left to lie, sometimes—"

"Damage!" I echoed stupidly. "What damage?"

He turned and gestured with a milk bottle. When you

come through our front gate you sweep round a tiny gravel drive which creates a half-moon of lawn, edged with flower beds nearest to the road. It was here that the white-coated milkman was pointing and I could see suddenly that all was not well.

I was barefoot. I ran wincing across the gravel. The flower beds had been trashed, my precious rose bushes hacked and torn. Scorched on the lawn, in capital letters a foot high, I saw the word BITCH.

"Mrs Donleavy?" I heard the milkman's voice fade as if he was moving rapidly away from me when, in fact, he was coming towards me. He grabbed me before I keeled over and I could hear Don's voice miles away asking, "What on earth's going on here?"

It had been many years since we had a village bobby, so Don reported the vandalism at Woodbridge police station. The following morning a red and white police car stopped in the lane and two young men in peaked caps rang the doorbell. The driver was blond and six feet tall, his partner was smaller and darker and a little older. He seemed to be in charge. They introduced themselves but their names didn't register; policemen are homogeneous. Nor did I do more than glance at their proffered warrant cards. I heard Don apologising for bringing them out over such a trivial matter and glared at him because it was no trivial matter to me.

The elder policeman, too, said politely that vandalism was a serious business and increasingly common even in this quiet neck of the woods. The blond one crouched on the lawn, testing the damage with a tentative finger. Then he stood up and looked over the fence.

"They didn't even have to come into the garden," he remarked. "They would have used some sort of weedkiller spray over the fence, and they could reach the roses easily." He looked down the lane. "Ashphalt. No prints. This road lead anywhere?"

"Just to some fields," Don said, "meadow land."

"So they took no risk at all, could have had it away at the first sign they'd been rumbled. Brave, aren't they?"

I stood feeling cold, staring at the dead garden. I gave a shiver. Don put his arm round my shoulder and I felt the reassuring pressure of his fingers in my flesh.

I saw that the letters were seeping now, as the weed-killer spread from the immediate attack area into the roots of the neighbouring grass blades. The movement was uneven and the letters looked like the Gothic title of some ancient Hammer horror coming shaking onto the screen, as if blood had been daubed on fresh plaster and left to drool. It wasn't red, of course, that *Bitch*, more brown, more rust.

"Bit of a mess," the older one said in distaste. "I ask you, what *is* the point?"

I invited them into the house and offered tea which they accepted. While they drank it we made our statement, two outraged householders.

"Have there been any other incidents?" the dark-haired one asked.

Don said, "No," as I simultaneously replied, "Yes."

"Well, which is it?" the blond one asked sharply.

I tried to tell them about Scamper and about the burnt hearthrug, but it came pouring out in a jumble so it sounded as if my puppy had caught fire one night. I saw the two policemen exchanging glances.

Don took charge calmly. "My wife lost her puppy recently, to a fox. And there was an incident when she went to sleep one night while I was away and forgot to put up the fireguard; all we lost that night was a hideous hearthrug. Just a couple of unrelated mishaps."

"No burglaries, break-ins, attempted break-ins?"

"None."

"No threats."

"Certainly not."

The policemen looked enquiringly at me, wondering no doubt if I would contradict this too. I closed my eyes, seeing the innocuous white envelopes with my name on them, or rather Don's name. I had destroyed the evidence. If I told them of the letters now, I couldn't prove that they'd ever existed, that they weren't a figment of my imagination.

"Any enemies?" one asked.

Don raised his eyebrows. "*Enemies*? What, like Tom Cruise, jealous because I'm a better actor than he is?"

The older man said, "Who isn't?" and the three of them enjoyed the joke.

The blond snapped his fingers. His young face, which until that moment had been impassive as only police faces can be, flushed with excitement. "Of course. I knew I recognised you. You're Captain Will Davenant. It's Will Davenant, Chris, from *Space Pirates*." Chris was carefully unimpressed and his friend added, "You haven't changed a bit, sir."

"Oh, I don't know about that," Don said modestly.

"I suspect it wasn't personal," Chris said after a moment. "We've had a bit of trouble round here lately with bikers: vandalism, theft, one young lad beaten up."

"Hell's Angels?" Don asked.

"I wouldn't call them that, sir. That would be to glamorise them. Just kids with no jobs and no brains and not enough to occupy their time. They get involved in petty crime, larceny, selling dope, mostly for money but sometimes – as in this case – for kicks."

He made it sound normal.

"Bitch," I said.

"Madam?"

"It was aimed at me. You don't call a man a bitch."

The one called Chris shrugged. "It was a fair guess that there would be a woman living here, nice country cottage, well-kept garden, two cars in the drive. Prosperous couple – symbols of everything they hate."

"They know they'll cause more distress to a woman, you see," his partner said.

"You didn't hear anything? Revving of bikes?" the older man resumed.

"Nothing," Don said when I didn't answer, "but our room is at the back."

He changed tack. "I see you're listed as having a shotgun licence, sir."

"Why, yes."

"So you actually keep a shotgun in the house?"

"I do, yes. I'd forgotten."

"Forgotten?"

"I can't remember the last time I took it out."

The older policeman looked alarmed. "But you do have it safely?"

"Of course, locked up in my study, unloaded."

"Only sometimes people get things out of proportion when it comes to their homes being in any way invaded, you see, sir, and when there's a weapon in the house . . . well, you see some kid scrumping an apple or swinging on the gate and, before you know what's happened, there's a shotgun or rifle being discharged at them. Only intended to scare them off, of course, but maybe the shot goes a bit awry. You can get into an awful lot of trouble that way."

"I promise you there'll be nothing like that. I used to do a bit of clay-pigeon shooting but, you know how it is, you take something up and then you get bored with it."

He hoped at one time that Colonel Apter might invite him on a pheasant shoot, make him part of the local gentry, but I don't think it even occurred to the old man.

"Oh, clay-pigeon shooting," the policeman said dismissively."I thought maybe you had it for protection, being a bit remote here, and we're not keen on that sort of thing."

Don gave them his most charming smile. “Strictly between ourselves, and please don’t tell the fans of Will Davenant, but I couldn’t hit a barn if I was standing inside it.”

“Which makes you more of a menace than someone who *can* shoot straight,” I murmured and he darted a hard look at me.

“You’ve kept up the licence, though,” Chris pointed out.

“Didn’t see any reason not to.”

“Fair enough. Think on what I said.”

Don showed them out, after he’d signed an autograph for the one who wasn’t called Chris. I stood in the hall as the three men walked slowly towards the gate. Through the open door I heard him say, “My wife hasn’t been altogether well lately and things do seem to have been piling up.” They nodded, looking back towards the house with sympathy, two young men, probably in their mid-twenties, young enough to be my sons. They knew about middle-aged women and their morbid fancies.

I tackled him as soon as he returned. “Why did you tell those boys I was ill?”

He looked astonished. “I was thinking of that ulcer of yours. Nasty things, ulcers.”

# Headless ghosts

Suza said that the landlord at the Old Piper had been complaining about bikers so I suggested that we walk across and have a word with him after lunch, to which she cheerfully agreed since she liked any excuse for a drink.

Half an hour later we were skirting the green. The Canada geese were standing on one leg by the pond as if it was a competition. I noticed wheel marks on the damp grass, circling wildly, deep tyre treads forming muddy tracks. We pushed open the door of the saloon bar, making a bell ring somewhere in the interior.

"Good morning, good morning," the landlord said although it was well after one. "Not often I see you two lovely ladies in here. Now, what can I get you?"

I gave him my brightest smile. I remembered how green his pleasant face had been after he'd shouldered down Miss Aspinall's front door that summer morning, releasing into the air a smell I hoped never to encounter again – the unalloyed decadence of death. I ordered a glass of mineral water, mindful of Bill's warnings about following a bland diet. Suza had a pint of Abbot's Ale.

I've never liked beer and am mildly envious of women who can down pints like men.

She also asked the landlord if he would have one himself, which is something women are never stupid enough to do. I mean, I don't go to the supermarket and tell the checkout girl to have a packet of tea bags on me. Obviously it was the right thing to do if we wanted information, but I would never have thought of it.

"That's very civil, Mrs Darc," the landlord said. "Don't mind if I do." He pulled a second pint. Then someone shouted through from the public bar and the landlord was gone before we could say anything, so we settled down at a table by the fire to await his return.

The pub had changed a lot in the eighties. When we first came to live in the village it was a shabby local, used by the people of Stratford and the neighbouring hamlet of Oldbourn, but there had not been enough profit in that for the brewery. The old landlord had been put out to grass and a new, younger man summoned from Bury St Edmunds to attract a clientele with deeper pockets. Now there were horse brasses on the walls and a real fire instead of the old log-effect electric job, and ten different types of wine available by the bottle and a happy hour from six till eight on Fridays and Saturdays.

"Greene King," Suza mused. "What is that? Some local legend, some eldritch ruler or Dark Age prince?"

"The brewery was started by a Mr Greene and Mr King," I replied. "Graham Greene's family." The Old Piper, on the other hand, *was* a local legend. No one ever looked properly at the signboard which stood across the road from the pub on the edge of the green. If they had they would have seen that the Piper was headless. Don't ask me how he can play the pipes without a head.

For some reason we're fond of headless ghosts in Suffolk. Leo's family have an entire phantom carriage with headless horses and footmen which appears, allegedly, on Christmas Eve. Everyone knows someone who knows someone whose grandfather saw it.

Suza looked at me severely over her glass, a line of froth clinging to her downy upper lip. "You're doing it again, Jennifer, seeking out the most prosaic, the most obvious answer. No, I like to think Ye Greene Kinge was some mythical tribal chieftain who stood out against the Roman invaders."

"Please yourself," I said tartly, "but my explanation is the true one."

"What is truth?"

The landlord came bustling back to his pint and Suza didn't stay for an answer. "I hear you've been having trouble with bikers lately, Terry," she called out instead.

"Ah yes," he said. "I heard about that business up at your place yesterday, Mrs Donleavy."

"Who from?"

"Two coppers came in this morning, asking about them bikers. They'd just come from your place."

"Talkative, aren't they?" I said, tight-lipped. If I wanted my misfortunes spread around the village I'd tell Mrs Price.

"And they like their beer," he said with a laugh. "Seriously, I told them straight: this is a nice class of pub, pretty view across the green, ducks and stuff on the pond. We get people out from Woodbridge and even Ipswich on a fine summer evening, as you know. The last thing I want is a load of scruffy bikers coming in and intimidating the regulars, but I can't refuse to serve them, 'less they're drunk already, like, so I makes them feel unwelcome and hopes they'll get the message and push off."

"Lucky you didn't get *your* garden trashed," I muttered.

"And when did these bikers come in last?" Suza asked.

"Night before last. Tuesday. Couple of them pissed in the bloody telephone box. Pardon my French, ladies. It's not like we haven't got toilets here!" The village had one of the old-style red phone boxes which are completely enclosed. BT had wanted to replace it with a perspex open one a couple of years ago, but we had got up a petition to stop them. It's that sort of village – had its red telephone box on the green since the Restoration, if you listen to some people.

"You must of heard them, Mrs Darc," the landlord went on. "They made enough racket with the bikes, silencers taken off and I don't know what, pampling over the green."

"When I'm working on my word processor at night," she said, "the roof could fall in and I wouldn't notice."

* * *

We got a letter from the police a week later, short and pointed. They regretted that in the current economic climate they were unable to devote any resources to the crime we'd reported.

## Repairing the damage

I wondered why Don kept peering out of the front window a couple of mornings after the attack. If I asked what he was looking for he would smile and say, "Nothing," or "I was wondering if the postman had been yet."

Finally, at half-past ten, a van stopped in the lane outside the house. It was white, open-sided as if it might be used for shifting livestock, and I could make out the words *Zebedee Landscapes* in moss green on the door. The van hooted with a feeble parp for its size and Don went out without a word to open the gate for them. They drove in onto the gravel and stopped. A young man got out of each side of the driver's cab and the one from the passenger side sprang forward to greet Don. They began to talk with some animation.

I found shoes and went out to join them. Aggie didn't follow but went to skulk in the kitchen. Lately my brave girl had become suspicious of strangers.

The man wasn't as young as I'd thought from a distance – mid-thirties, perhaps. He had light brown hair pulled back into a ponytail. His skin was tanned the dark brown achieved only by someone who works in the open air, and his blue eyes blazed out of a web of crinkles.

He turned towards me as I reached them, his body language politely including me in the conversation. "No," he was saying. "We had no trouble finding the place at all."

He wore jeans and a short-sleeved shirt and a sleeveless padded jacket with bulging pockets both inside and outside. A blue and white scarf was knotted with studied casualness round his throat. He was well over six feet tall and thin and stood with his hands on his hips, surveying the garden. He looked revoltingly healthy, as if he'd been fed on best corn from the cradle.

"My wife," Don said.

His voice, when he greeted me, was unexpected, pure public school. "Hugh Aysgarth," he said, "and this is my assistant, John."

The younger man didn't speak but made a sort of half bow of acknowledgement in my direction. He was shorter and stockier than his boss, had blond hair cropped short and a ruddy face with pale blue eyes. He wore overalls atop a greying T-shirt and trainers. He stood with his hands in his pockets, docilely waiting.

Aysgarth turned to look at the lawn, which was now almost totally black. "No need to ask where the damage is!" he said. "What on earth happened?"

"Bikers," Don said. "Sheer vandalism."

"On an innocent garden," Aysgarth said. "It makes you want to weep." I noticed that he had the most enormous feet, literally a foot long in their old but well-tended Timberland shoes. "Well," he said, "we'll make a start on clearing the ruined turf first. John?"

John went wordlessly to the back of the van, took out a formidable spade and began to etch straight lines on the dead grass, dissecting it into patches about a foot square. I saw sleek muscles flexing in both his hairless arms. In the few minutes while we stood and watched him he had neatly dug up a dozen squares and piled them on the path.

"Quick, isn't he?" Aysgarth said. "You'll have a new lawn by the end of the week, Mrs Donleavy. Bit of time for the turf to settle and you'll never know there was ever anything wrong." He turned to the flower bed and stroked his chin where a few barbs of pale stubble showed fashionably.

"What I'd like you to do," Don said, "if that's okay, Hugh, is to grub up these ruined rose bushes as soon as possible, so my wife doesn't have to look at them any more. I'll burn them on the bonfire round the back, get rid of all trace of them."

"Okay. No problem." Aysgarth glanced at me with compassion. I wasn't sure that Don was right. Perhaps I needed time to grieve.

"Then we'll get the soil in the best possible condition for replanting," Don went on. "Really treat it. We've got a big bin of compost happily rotting out the back and there can hardly be a shortage of horse manure round these parts."

"Goat dung," Aysgarth said. "Every time. I know a man with goats."

Ashes, I thought. That was the thing for roses.

"Look on the bright side," Aysgarth said. "It's exactly the right time of the year for planting roses. If you get cracking and decide what varieties you want and John and I get the beds prepared, as you say, you'll have a wonderful show in the spring."

"Good," Don said, when I didn't speak.

"What was this?" He fingered the remains of a bush. "Old Blush China?"

"The last rose of summer," I said softly, "left blooming alone." I caught Don's eye and shrugged defensively. "That's what they call it."

"And the Rosa Mundi," Aysgarth went on, exploring. "My favourite."

I warmed to him. "Mine too."

"Peau Douce; soft as a baby's . . . cheek."

I laughed for the first time since the milkman rang the bell.

"Do you make pot pourri?" he asked me.

"Oh, yes, and rose-petal sorbet."

"I've never had that. I'd like to try it."

"Next time I make a batch, I'll let you know."

"I'll get the pH balance checked," he said. "He reached into the glove compartment of his cabin and extracted a small polythene bag, like the ones banks use for holding coins. Then he took a clean trowel and scooped up some earth, put it in the bag and sealed it. "Roses incline to an acid soil," he said, as if I might not know that. "Which is probably what you've got anyway."

"I've never had any trouble getting roses to grow here," I said.

He gave me a brilliant smile. "By the time we've finished with this soil, Mrs Donleavy, your new roses will be the pride of Suffolk."

"Would you like a cup of tea?" I asked, since there seemed to be nothing left for me to do.

John spoke for the first time. He said, "Two sugars, please."

"Where did you get them from?" I asked Don as I was making the tea.

"*Les Pages Jaunes*, of course. Where do you think?"

"They're not the people Suza used?"

"I don't know. I didn't enquire."

"But why them in particular?"

"Don't you like them? You've only just met them."

"I do like them, but they're not quite what I would expect."

"No, Hugh's not exactly your horny-handed son of earth, is he?" He put on a comic Mummerset voice. "Rambling Sid Rumpole – the aarnsa loies in the soil." Reverting to normal, he added, "Funny the things people turn their hands to these days. Beats sitting behind a desk, I suppose, and at least you're your own boss. To answer your question, they were the last ones listed: Zebedee."

"Trust you," I said. "Most people pick Aardvark—"

"Aardvark Landscapes?" he interrupted. "Ve vark aarder?"

"Funny, aren't you?"

"I like to think so."

"Everything's a joke to you, isn't it, Don?"

He sighed. "Not everything, dear heart, but you take things far too seriously. The damage can be repaired, and right speedily."

"Only the physical damage."

"Yes," he said. "All right. But let's keep things in perspective, shall we? No one has died. No one is injured."

"And do we need professionals?"

My husband looked at me in mock dismay. "My dear Jennifer, you don't seriously expect me to *dig*, myself? In the garden? With a spade? To risk calluses? Why, I would never be able to start a second career as a hand model!"

He examined his hands smugly. They were small for a man's. He got them manicured regularly, which my father would have called plain effeminate, but then he'd had trouble getting used to the idea that Don had to wear make-up to work.

I noticed that his wedding ring was loose where he'd lost weight, pushing easily up against the knuckle of his third finger. It had to be loose enough to remove, since Captain Will Davenant and his like clearly weren't the marrying kind, but now he might lose it if he wasn't careful.

"Aren't they expensive, though?" I persisted.

"Yes, well. A bit. I rang Gloria and told her I'd do that

insurance advert after all. The pay's pretty good. Enough to cover Hugh and his taciturn friend."

He'd been offered the leading role – if you can call it that in a thirty-second commercial – in an advertisement for Surefire Insurance. They wanted him to be a middle-aged man who, on being introduced to his first grandchild at the hospital, realises that he's no longer young and begins to brood on whether he has made adequate pension provision.

*You can be sure with Surefire.*

Don had refused it, not on the grounds that it struck a little close to home, as you might imagine, but that he thought himself too young for the role. He was, apparently, oblivious to the irony of this.

Every year I have to remind him to put as much as we can afford into a pension plan.

"They'd want me to wear one of those shiny car coats," he'd said with a shiver of distaste. But now it seemed he was prepared to endure anything, even his fans seeing him in a car coat, to repair my garden.

I flung my arms round him and gave him a great big kiss and he said, "Hey, hey! What's this?" and, nodding out of the window towards the gardeners, "*Pas devant les domestiques!*"

# Apple tree

At half-past twelve I saw Aysgarth stroll round to the back of the house and stretch out on the wooden bench under the magnolia. He pulled a square packet of aluminium foil from one of his bulging pockets, unwrapped it and took out a sandwich.

He ate it daintily, in nibbles. When he'd eaten half of it he put the rest down carefully on the arm of the bench, took a packet of cigarettes from another pocket and lit one.

I went out to join him. He waved the cigarette. "You don't mind? I thought in the garden—"

"I don't mind at all," I said.

I'd got used to it, since Don had smoked in all the twenty-five years I'd known him. In fact it seemed strange now he'd finally given up after so many abortive attempts. The rooms smelt fresher, the walls stayed cleaner and Suza no longer had to wheeze pointedly every time he lit up.

"I could do a lot with this," Aysgarth said, gesturing round the back garden. "It's a good shape, a good size – unusual without being eccentric."

"I like it fairly wild," I said defensively.

"Oh, sure! You don't want a bijou cottage garden with the flowers bullied into regimented rows. I hate that. Sometimes I have to provide it but I hate it. It's like keeping animals in cages."

"Not really, surely." The flower and vegetable liberation front?

He smiled. "Well, perhaps not really." He gestured at the thick yew hedge that grew some six feet high and twenty feet across. "That's not the bottom of the garden?"

"No. Beyond it is the kitchen garden, the compost heap and the bonfire."

"Neatly camouflaged? Good."

"I grow a few vegetables," I said, "leeks, courgettes, peppers, runner beans – but mostly herbs."

"Ah, you're the village wise woman, perhaps?"

Had he just called me a witch? "For cooking."

His eyes traversed the scene, missing nothing, and finally fell on the mounds under the apple tree.

"Animal cemetary?" I nodded. "That's good. Earth to earth, ashes to ashes. Nothing like a bit of bone meal for the soil. From abattoir to garden. It's so neat, so clever. So *meant*." I thought of the plastic carrier bag that swaddled Scamper's body and felt guilty. "I notice there's a touch of fungus on the apple tree," he said.

"Where?" I jumped to my feet.

"About two feet from the ground." He pointed. "Do

you see? That whitish haze. Leave it with me. I'll get it sorted before we go. Catch it before it takes hold."

"Thanks." It seemed that Hugh Aysgarth was going to earn his keep.

"Are they good apples?"

"Yes. Red eaters, little but sweet."

Actually they were red on one side and green on the other, like the one Snow White was given by her wicked stepmother.

Hugh resumed his sandwich. John came round the corner carrying – carefully, since both had hefty thorns – two dead rose bushes. He looked at us in silent query and Aysgarth said, "Behind there," pointing at the yew hedge. The younger man disappeared for two minutes then came back empty-handed. This pantomime continued until the ruined roses were piled on the bonfire waiting for a firelighter and a match.

Meanwhile Hugh Aysgarth finished his sandwiches, ate a pear, smoothed out his aluminium foil, folded it into a fat square and put it back in his pocket. He smoked another cigarette.

As John came past for the last time, Aysgarth said, "Take a break now, John, why don't you?" The boy wiped his hands on the thighs of his overalls and sat on the stone parapet that separates the paved area from the garden. Both men looked at me expectantly.

"I'll go and make some more tea," I said.

It was, of course, Aysgarth who answered. "That'd be lovely, Mrs Donleavy. Thank you."

By the end of the day the lawn was also gone, piled in the back of the van, and the two men drove it away, promising fresh turf for the morrow.

# Secrets

I was in Ipswich on Tuesday afternoon, browsing among the market stalls, examining bric-a-brac, when I heard someone calling my name. It was Penny Gammon. I was genuinely glad to see her and we exchanged greetings.

She looked at her watch and said, "How about a cup of tea?" to which I agreed. I put down the small porcelain dog I'd been holding. It was overpriced and Don said we had too much rubbish in the house already. The stallholder gave Penny a dirty look since he knew a soft touch when he saw one and didn't see why it should be whisked away by a fat woman in a flowery print frock and a duffel coat.

Soon we were safely settled in our seats in a small tea shop off the Butter Market and had ordered a pot of Darjeeling for two.

"I'm surprised your great friend Suza isn't with you," Penny said.

"We don't live in each other's pockets," I protested.

"How's the ulcer?" she asked. "Oops!" She put her hand over her mouth. "I'm not supposed to know about that, am I? I shall get that husband of mine struck off one of these days."

I laughed. "I'm not ashamed of having an ulcer. It'd be a different story if it was syphilis."

"My dear! I would burst having to keep a secret like that."

"Seriously, I feel heaps better."

"Those modern drugs are marvellous. It was only a few years ago, once you got an ulcer you were likely as not stuck with it for life. These days – shazam! – six weeks of pill popping and it's gone." She turned round and eyed a plate of cakes. "Perhaps I can be pressed to one of those chocolate truffle concoctions." She gestured for the waitress.

"You never have any trouble with your digestive organs?" I said enviously.

"Damn right! Cast-iron stomach, Bill says. No, if I suddenly got the guts ache, I'd know old Bill was trying to poison me."

"I don't know how anyone could do that to me," I said. "Practically everything I eat I cook myself."

"Doesn't the lovely Don even bring you up an early morning cuppa?"

"Are you kidding? Other way round."

"And doesn't he ever take you out for a meal? You let him take you for granted, Jenny."

"There's nowhere much to go round here," I said apologetically. "I sit there thinking how much better I could have done it myself and grudging the expense."

"That's not the point. It's nice for a woman to be waited on hand and foot occasionally and not have the whole meal spooked by the thought of the washing up. Oh, look!" She banged on the window, making the waitress glare. "Old Colonel Apter," she explained. "He didn't see me."

"You find just about everybody you know in Ipswich on a Tuesday afternoon," I said, thinking of the increasing number of white envelopes that found their way onto my fire.

# Absence

Although I'd had my copy of Suza's new book for a month it was just being published in late November. She went to London for the launch at the same time that Don was away doing the Surefire commercial. I suppose I'd hoped she might invite me to the party, which was at the Groucho Club, but she didn't mention it and I didn't like to ask. Perhaps she had one life in Suffolk and a different life in London. Perhaps I would seem hopelessly provincial to her London friends.

It would have been an opportunity to wear my new outfit, I thought wistfully, since such occasions seemed likely to be thin on the ground.

Don was staying at Toby's flat again and rang me each evening.

"How's the car coat?" I asked the first time.

"Actually they put me in a tweed jacket, which was okay. Only then, when I'd seen my grandson, I had to change into a woolly cardi!" I could almost hear him shuddering. "I ask you. I shall never be able to hold my head up in public again. At least they decided I haven't enough grey hair; they've silvered my temples."

I giggled. "I'm sure you look very distinguished."

"That's a euphemism for old. I wish I was dead."

"Give it time, old dear, give it time."

"Thanks very much."

I heard the doorbell ring in the background, a two-tone chime: *bing, bong*. "That'll be my pizza."

"You sent out for pizza!" That didn't sound like Don. I'd assumed he'd spend the evening carousing in some restaurant with other thesps.

"The small 'diet' pizza, and some salad. I'm too tired to do anything other than slump on the sofa in front of the TV. I really am getting old, you know."

*Bing, bong.*

"I'd better answer it. Talk to you tomorrow."

When Suza returned the following day she looked tired and a little pale.

"I would rather walk for miles than be interviewed by the press, far less exhausting," she said. "They ask you what the book is *about*, even though they're supposed to have read it; and what they mean is 'Tell me the plot' which is not at all the same thing as what the book is *about*. And I never sleep well these days when I'm away from home. God! I'm turning into a right moaner. How have you been, my love?"

"Oh fine. I'd have thought it would make a nice change," I commented.

She looked up, comprehension passing clearly across

her face. “Oh, Jen! Did you want to come? I never thought. Since I consider it a chore and a bore myself, it simply didn’t occur to me that anyone as sane as you would *want* to inflict it on herself.”

“I expect it’s a lot like a first-night party,” I said. “Or an end-of-filming bash.”

“I imagine so.”

“Well, I’ve been to loads of them.” Although not recently.

Interviews, it seemed, could be expected in *The Times*, the *Independent* and the *Guardian*.

# Cobwebs

It was a foggy morning: what we in Suffolk call a cobweb morning. I woke early as I do when Don isn't there in the bed beside me. We've seldom been able to arrange to get newspapers delivered so that we can read them cosily in bed over early-morning tea. The milkman tried it for six months but he complained that people were always changing their order or cancelling at the last minute and leaving him with unsold copies on his hands, so the experiment didn't last.

Mrs Price now ordered our *Times* and one of us – meaning me – would walk down to the village in the morning to get it. And today was the day that the first of Suza's interviews was due to appear.

I made Aggie her breakfast of scrambled egg with a piece of brown bread soaked in milk. I made do with some toast. When she'd cleaned the bowl I called, "Walkies," and she went off to fetch her lead.

You can't usually walk into fog: it retreats before you like a rainbow, but not this morning. I had an odd feeling that it might be like in *The Midwich Cuckoos* where the whole village is sealed off from the outside world for a few hours and that if I tried to walk away from the centre, towards Woodbridge, I might come up against an impenetrable barrier. We knew our route, though, and walked quickly up the lane onto the road and followed it for the last quarter mile into the village.

"You're out and about early, Mrs Donleavy." Mrs Price reached for my paper as soon as I came in the door. I was the only customer. "Nasty old morning."

I agreed that it was and tucked the paper under my arm.

Pauline Price was about my age, perhaps even a year or two younger, but somehow I never thought of her as belonging to the same generation as me. I was a bohemian actor and she was a middle-aged woman who went to work every day in a clean wrap-around pinny and sensible shoes. I couldn't imagine her swinging in the seventies. She surely was born for an earlier age of beehive hairdos and nice girls who didn't.

"How do you fare today?" she asked, as she usually did.

"Quite well, thank you." I knew I couldn't get out of the place without an exchange of village news, while *The Times* was burning a hole in my armpit. "Oh, can I have a couple of first-class stamps while I'm here?"

"The post office isn't open yet, of course, but if it's plain stamps you're wanting I've got one of those books of four I can let you have."

"That will be fine."

"Now, where are they? That's the question."

As she fussed about looking for them, opening and closing drawers ineffectually, she remarked, "Got a new pen pal, have you?"

"I beg your pardon?"

"Only Stan, the postman, was saying, this morning, as you been getting a lot more letters lately."

"What's that supposed to mean?" I snapped.

"Well." She looked taken aback. "He was just saying that the letters at the White House are mostly for *Mr* Donleavy, but that you must have a new pen pal as has been writing to you lately. Just passing the time of day, like. No offence meant."

"He's got no business nosing into my letters!" I yelled. "And you are . . . you are . . . a fucking evil, interfering, gossiping old bitch!"

It was as though a cloak of silence had fallen over the village and the birds had stopped singing. I was sure there wasn't a house where they weren't lifting their noses from their breakfast cups to ask each other, "What was that noise? Did someone really say *fuck* to Mrs Price?" I was as stunned as she was. I felt my cheeks glowing red. I wouldn't apologise. I would not. Was it her? Was this part of the plot? Who more likely to be writing anonymous letters than this inquisitive, prurient, prying, meddlesome . . . harmless, well-meaning old woman?

Mrs Price set her lips in a straight line and said, "That'll be thirty pee for the paper, Mrs Donleavy, and I have asked you before not to let that smelly old dog follow you into my shop. 'Tisn't hygienic." Clearly I wasn't going to get any stamps, not any more.

I fumbled in my pocket and slammed a fifty-pence piece down on the counter. I didn't wait for my change. I heard her breathe "Well!" as Aggie and I slammed out of the shop.

Outside there was a big blurred circle of yellow low in the sky as the sun did battle with the fog. There were no lights on at Madder Cottage, no sign of life anywhere. The church bell struck the half-hour. I began to run, back the way I'd come, along the deserted road, down the lane, Aggie barking joyfully at my heels, enjoying her unaccustomed frolic.

I banged through the gate and took a short cut across the rose beds and the new lawn despite Hugh's strict instructions not to walk on it until further notice. I wrestled with the front door and sank down heavily at the kitchen table. I realised there was an unholy mess on my shoes from the treated soil – well-rotted shit, bone meal, ashes from the burnt bushes and dried blood.

Aggie nosed round my feet, excited by the foul smell, and I swatted her with the newspaper. She retired to her basket with a reproachful look. Was there anyone I wasn't capable of offending that morning? "You're not smelly," I told her. "You don't want to take any notice of that old bitch." Though a canine presumably wouldn't consider 'bitch' to be a term of abuse.

I sat quietly waiting for my heartbeat, my breathing, to return to normal. I was wheezing the way Suza does when something triggers off an asthma attack. I made a fresh pot of coffee. I heard the post plop through the letter box but couldn't bring myself to go and pick it up in case there was one of those hateful white envelopes. How dare they? How dare Stan go around telling people I seldom got any letters? How dare they talk about me behind my back?

I shook the paper open and turned to the features page. A photo of Suza caught my eye at once, taking up a quarter of the broadsheet page. She was wearing a pale blouse that I hadn't seen before, opened low to show a hint of cleavage. Lipstick enhanced her generous mouth. She looked sexy and powerful and I felt proud of her.

I forced a smile onto my lips, as I had found in the past that this can actually lift my mood. In the early days when I had to do things like the Motor Show and the Ideal Home Exhibition to make ends meet between acting jobs, I'd learnt to smile from dawn till dusk without a hint of strain. In fact, I would often arrive home with the grin plastered on my face, as if I'd simply forgotten to remove it, and Don would ask, "What's tickling you?"

"Nothing," I would say, "but you can."

I sipped some hot coffee with cream and began to read.

Five minutes later I put the paper down again, shaken and bewildered.

# Fiction

"I don't understand," I said.

It was lunchtime and I was in the kitchen at Madder Cottage. Suza had taken some quiches out of the freezer and was about to put them in the microwave.

I flourished the paper. I said, "It says here that you're a widow."

She shrugged. "You expect me to tell some half-baked journo, barely out of nappies, that my husband left me for a surveyor called Tom? Of course I lie to them."

"Was he the one from Acton?" I asked. "Tom?"

"Mmm? He lived in Hounslow or somewhere equally dreary. Why Acton?"

"The one your husband was arrested with," I persisted. "In the gents."

"Oh, that. No."

I saw it now. I felt stupid. "You made that up too – that stuff about him being arrested for cottaging. Didn't you? You want to get your stories straight, Suza, remember what you told to who."

"Whom."

"Don't correct my grammar!" I flourished the paper at her some more. "It says here you had no education, left school at fifteen."

"Your point?" She put the quiches in the microwave and set the timer.

"When you were playing bridge at our house you said you'd played for your college."

"Sit down, Jenny. I don't know what you're upsetting yourself about. One never tells the truth to journalists. They distort everything one says, anyway, to suit their own slant, so why bother? The *Guardian* will have got a completely different story. There I will be a cosy, dreary housewife living in a picture-book cottage—"

"What? Like me?"

"—scribbling novels at the kitchen table when I've finished darning hubby's socks. In the *Independent* I shall probably be an ex-nun."

"Don't they mind when they finally compare notes and find you've been taking the piss?"

"Too damn late!"

"How can I know what the truth is, Suza? How do I know that everything you've told *me* isn't a lie?"

"Because you're my friend."

"Am I? How can I trust you? How can I trust in anything that has passed between us all these months, when I've been opening my heart to you and thought you were doing the same; while all the time your bits were – what? – short stories?"

She looked amused. "More like a collection of poems."

The microwave pinged. "I live in a world of imagination, Jenny. It's my job."

"More like a fantasy world," I said coldly.

"That only applies to people who can't tell the difference – between fantasy and reality."

"And you're sure *you* can? Do you know what I think, Suza?"

"No, but I dare say you're going to tell me."

"I think that you had a normal, averagely happy, middle-class upbringing, like me, like millions of other people. I think that your dad – and I bet he was your *real* dad – didn't hit you, that you didn't run away from home as soon as you were eighteen. I think that you and your husband drifted apart the way other couples do; but that isn't exotic enough for you, isn't *interesting* enough, so you make something up, like you made up your stupid name."

She took a quiche out and poked it in the middle. "Needs a couple more minutes."

"Stuff it," I said. "You can stuff your lousy food and you can stuff your 'friendship'."

It seemed that Suza had not simply a life in London and a life in Suffolk, as I'd thought, but any number of different lives, virtual lives, available for her to use as it suited her.

When I was fifteen I had a serious crush on a sixth-form boy called Joe Tyler. It was the mid-sixties and he had a Beatles haircut, strongly disapproved of by the headmaster, which made him a romantic rebel. I was always looking for excuses to hang around the sixth-form common room hoping for a glimpse of him. If I came across him unexpectedly in the course of the school day, my heart would literally go pitt-a-pat.

Once I found him and another boy skulking round the back of the changing rooms when they were supposed to be playing football. They were smoking, inexpertly, and I stood gazing in awe at this flagrant breach of school rules until Joe said, "Hey, small fry, fuck off out of it." So I did. His rudeness didn't make me love him any the less, rather the reverse.

I found out where he lived, not far from me, and would hang around outside his house when I was supposed to be doing my homework, seeing the lights come on in his bedroom, hearing the music played inconsiderately loud: The Stones, Gerry and the Pacemakers, Elvis and, of course, The Beatles.

He lived in a council house and his father was a dustman in the days before they were called refuse collectors. He was my one and only attempt at a bit of rough trade.

Then, one Saturday, when I happened to be passing, as usual, I saw him and a group of his cronies throwing stones at a dog. They'd tied it to a post on a piece of waste ground so it couldn't get away and it was twisting and whining and snapping.

My love died, completely and irrevocably. I saw a tall gangly bully with adolescent acne on his chin and a hairdo that didn't suit him, with a sullen expression and a foul mouth.

And I despised us both.

It seemed I was destined to come home fuming that day. Aggie greeted me at the door with her brush in her mouth and I realised that I hadn't groomed her for ages. And wondered how I could have been so forgetful. I locked the front door behind me. I never used to do that during the day while I was at home but it seemed essential now. I made a fuss of her and she followed me into the kitchen.

The phone rang while I was grooming her, gently since her old skin wasn't so supple these days. The machine wasn't on and I let it ring. I think it hardly occurred to me to answer. It rang perhaps ten times, then stopped. Then a minute later it rang again, for about six rings this time.

Why do people do that? Do they think I'm more likely to answer the second time?

I finished her off with a piece of black velvet, polishing her coat to silk. There was something soothing about the regular motion. Then she went out into the garden and rolled in the mud.

# Liar, liar

Don came home without warning late that evening. I hadn't expected him back until the weekend. "I wanted to see you," he said with his easy smile. "I can get the commuter train in the morning."

"I don't believe you," I said. Straight out, just like that. I'd never called him a liar to his face before.

He finally admitted that Suza had telephoned him.

"How did she come to have the number of Toby's flat?" I wanted to know.

"I gave it to her, obviously."

"Why?"

"Because I asked her to keep an eye on you while I was away. Okay?"

"No, it is not fucking okay." He stared at me since I never swore, or not *that* word, anyway. "I'm an adult woman, competent and sane, and people keep talking to me as if I was incapable, as if I was ill, and I'm so sick of people talking about me behind my back."

"You *have* been ill—"

"I've had a fucking ulcer! Like a zillion other people.

And it's better now. I haven't had a pain for . . . well, for ages. Ask Bill if you don't believe me."

"Also . . ." He cleared his throat. "Suza said something about an incident in the village shop this morning. It seems you were effing and blinding at Mrs Price. I didn't believe it at first, but now I'm not so sure . . . Jennifer?"

I might have known that Mrs Price wouldn't keep any of that to herself. I can imagine her, hear her. *You'll never believe what that Mrs Donleavy said to me this morning. Off her head, if you ask me. And such* language! *I thought she was a regular lady. She's an actress, of course. Probably no better than she should be.*

Why need any of us be better than we should be?

The whole village must know by now.

"Jenny," he said, "please."

"Please what?"

"You're not well. I want you to go back and see Bill, talk to him."

"Oh, I'll bet," I said. "Tell me something, Don."

"Yes?"

"Why did you ever marry me? Why me, when there were so many prettier, cleverer, sexier girls waiting to fall into your lap? You could have done so much better for yourself; God knows, your mother made that plain to me often enough."

*But who is she? Who are her people? What does her father do? An assistant bank manager? At Barclays? I see. I trust it will be a long engagement, Andrew; you are so young.* That was how the news of me was greeted by my ever-loving mother-in-law. *I hope this girl isn't trying to . . .* trap *you in marriage, Andrew.*

Meaning had he got me in the club?

Fat chance.

He ran his hand over his face. He looked old suddenly, old enough to be worrying about his Surefire pension. I saw that the recent weight loss had added new lines to his face. In the end he evidently decided to take my question at face value.

"A, because I loved you; B, because you were the first person I'd ever met who was prepared to love *me* unconditionally, not like my mother who wanted me to *succeed*, and pass exams and have a mortgage and an overdraft, and be a credit to her; not like other girls who sized me up with their greedy eyes. Will he be rich and famous? Is he a good each-way bet?"

I made to speak, although I don't know what I would have said, but he silenced me with a gesture of his hands. "I saw you watching me and I could see that you loved me and that you would support me and hold me in your arms when I was afraid and that you would love me when I was old. I can be myself with you. I don't have to pretend. I don't have to be witty and amusing and handsome all the time. I don't have to be swashbuckling Captain Will Davenant. I can be dull and tired and stupid, like now."

I was silent, chastened. He'd come rushing back from London because he cared. Then I said, "Pour yourself a small whisky while I run you a quick bath. Then we'll get some sleep. I'll drive you to the station in the morning."

He got obediently up. Everything was normal again.

"I have always wanted you to succeed," I said.

"Yes, I know, but for my sake, not your own." He yawned and stretched, then gave a start of surprise. "What's that doing there?" He picked up the photo from the study that was propped up on the table. "Where did this come from?"

"It hangs on the wall of the study," I said.

"Oh, yeah, so it does. I'd forgotten about it. Don't see it any more. Don't I look young?"

"The picture hook came down," I lied. "I'll put a new one up tomorrow."

"Hardly worth it." He went across to the drinks cabinet and took out a bottle of malt. He poured himself a fingerful and said casually, "Tomorrow morning, nip round and make it up with Suza. Eh?"

"Can't," I said. "I'm going riding with Leo Apter."

So there.

# Invitation to the dance

A white envelope was lying on the mat.

I stepped over it as I got back from the station and looked down at it. I turned it over with my foot to see the front. It was squarer than the usual letters and the address was handwritten in swirling italic in black ink: Mr and Mrs Andrew Donleavy.

I laughed and picked it up. It was the annual invitation to Mr Herzog's At Home. It was on the second Saturday in December and everybody in the neighbouring villages was invited and it was pretty much the high spot of the social year. He served excellent champagne and we always went.

I slit it open and took out a white card edged with gold. I ran my finger over the real engraving; Mr Herzog liked to do things in style. We were expected to RSVP in the third person, on good quality writing paper, handwritten: Mr and Mrs Andrew Donleavy will be pleased to attend . . .

I had turned the envelope over in my hand and something unexpected caught my eye and interrupted my train of thought. It bore an Ipswich postmark. This surprised me. Mr Herzog had no car and seldom left the village, ordering up a chauffeur-driven Bentley for special occasions. Surely he would post his invitations in the postbox by the green, outside Mrs Price's shop. Why should he bother to go to Ipswich to post them?

The anonymous letters were postmarked Ipswich, on a Tuesday afternoon, which was market day, the most populous day of the week. I had assumed that my "well-wisher" went into town that day, as I did myself.

But what if . . . what if?

The clock struck half-past eight. I put the invitation on the table to reply to later and went upstairs and changed into my jodhpurs.

If Leo had been surprised to receive my call after so many months, she hid it well. She'd agreed readily to come riding with me that morning and was on the doorstep of Stratford House before I'd even switched off my engine. A skittish Labrador ran barking at me as I got out of the car but was hushed and sent back inside in disgrace.

The house was early Georgian and a bit austere for my tastes: straight, regular, symmetrical. Leo lived there with her mother and father, both elderly now. They were an old Suffolk family, the local gentry, well enough off, although the house was kept on the cool side in cold weather. They did the things that the country gentry do: kept horses, even went shooting in the winter, and Leo unsentimentally followed the hunt.

She was a small creature, elfin, but wiry and strong, no

doubt from having spent half her life on a pony since she was three. She was fair of hair and skin, preserving her oval face from the ravages of the sun. She looked younger than she was but then she'd never been married, or even left home, and her worries must be few.

She asked no questions about my long absence but said, "It's nice to see you, Jennifer," and gave me a peck on the cheek. As I followed her towards the stables she asked, "How are you?"

"Fine. You?"

"I've been frantically busy, what with the poetry festival, but that's over now and we're due for a bit of a fallow period."

"Of course, you have that to contend with now as well as the music festival."

There's something about *poets*," she said.

"You're allergic to them?"

She laughed. "I sometimes think I may be! To all writers. They're so *self-centred*." She took my arm. "I'm glad you're able to come riding with me again."

"Yes," I said. "So am I."

We rode miles, out through Rendlesham forest. It was the end of autumn and the dead leaves mulched beneath our feet. It was a bumper year for toadstools, swelling like miniature umbrellas under the trees, exploding at the touch of a hoof. You could see the horses' breath on the air at first but soon the sun burnt away the last of the mist.

My mare, Foxtrot, was eager and strained at the bit. It

took all my strength to keep control of her. I wondered how Suza could dislike horses with their wonderful power and grace, their satin skin and wise eyes.

"She's not been getting enough exercise lately," Leo said, noticing. "Georgie hasn't been home much to take her for a run."

Georgie was her brother, a big, kindly, not very bright man of forty, who lived in London but usually came home at weekends. A few generations ago he'd have been sent out to run some distant colony; now he worked in a merchant bank.

"Is he courting?" I asked.

She laughed at the old-fashioned expression. "Perhaps he is. Mummy mutters occasionally that it's time he settled down but I think she's secretly given up hope of both of us."

We stopped at the top of a small hill to let the horses catch their breath. I knew my muscles would ache tomorrow but it was worth it. I could see clean across the flat land I'd come to love.

"I see you've had Hugh Aysgarth in to repair your garden," she remarked.

"You know him?"

"Sure, he was at school with Georgie. I've known him since I was a little girl." She grimaced. "Another *old Suffolk family*."

"And do they approve of him taking up gardening?"

"Not much, but then he never sticks at anything for long. He gets enthusiastic about something for a few months, then he's off after some other novelty. Same with women."

Was there a personal sour note there? I didn't ask. I'd never had that *intimacy* with any girlfriend before Suza, but what you've never had you never miss. Instead I said, "He seems to know his stuff."

"Oh, yes. He's very plausible. Between ourselves, the Aysgarths are unstable. Still, I expect they say the same thing about the Apters. If you ask me, Hugh is a few rolled oats short of a nose bag."

"His friend doesn't say much."

"Who, John? The Borstal boy?"

"What?"

"That's where Hugh got him, out of Hollesley. Didn't you know?"

Hollesley Bay Colony was a young offender's institute a few miles away on the coast.

I was shaken. "No, I had no idea."

"Don't you believe in rehabilitation?" Leo asked slyly.

"Of course, in theory."

"But not in your back garden?"

I gave myself a mental shake and told myself firmly that it was good and noble of Hugh to give the boy a job.

Or was he just cheap?

"What was he in for?" I asked cautiously.

She shrugged. "It's not the sort of question you can ask. The usual boyish things, I expect: fighting, shoplifting. Even Georgie used to go pilfering when he was a teenager; they dare each other. The one time he got caught the shopkeeper told Daddy instead of the police. I think Georgie would have preferred the police. Daddy can be . . . magisterial. Don't look so worried. They grow out of it." I hoped so.

"Did you hear Daddy shot a fox?" Leo went on.

"Shot it? The Colonel? Isn't that a bit . . . ?

"Ungentlemanly? A bit, but needs must when the devil drives. It was a big old dog fox that had been killing our birds and even terrorising our dogs, far too wily ever to succumb to the hounds."

So my remaining dog was safe. It seemed time to change the subject. "Do you know anything about the post?" I asked.

"I'm not with you."

"If I post a letter on the village green is it postmarked Stratford St James?"

"I don't think so," she said slowly. "I think everything is piled into a van and taken to Ipswich and sorted and stamped there."

"So, as long as it's within the Ipswich catchment area, there's no way of knowing where a letter was posted."

"I think that's right." She gave me a sideways look. "Do you want me to ask Mrs Price for you?"

I felt myself redden. "You heard, then?"

"My dear! There's no one this side of the Deben who hasn't heard. It was high time someone told Mrs Price where to get off. Well done!"

I accepted her offer and we stopped on the green on the way back. I held her horse while she went into the shop. Foxtrot began to eat mouthfuls of grass that looked muddy to me but I let her get on with it. I had my back to Madder Cottage, looking resolutely into the well-tended garden of the Old Rectory. I saw Mr Herzog coming out of the door and he waved. I waved back. I wouldn't dream of breaching etiquette by yelling that we gladly accepted his invitation.

Leo reappeared after five minutes and confirmed that postal stamping was now done centrally. She didn't once ask why I wanted to know and I was grateful for her discretion.

So the letters could have been posted here, on the village green, or in any one of a dozen local villages. It could be any one of my friends and neighbours: Mr Herzog, Mrs Price, Penny Gammon, Claire Cross, Leo Apter.

An autumn breeze blew through the willows by the pond. I listened but it didn't whisper the name of my enemy.

## Does it matter *whose* story it is?

"Have I told you the one about the time I was appearing at the Chichester Festival with Joan Plowright?" Don asked Suza one lunchtime.

Yes, we'd made it up. Things would never be the same but we both pretended that they were, the way a man and wife struggle on for the sake of appearances, not admitting that love had died.

Don had reminded me how angry and upset I'd been when newspapers and magazines intruded on us in the *Space Pirates* era. I'd been angry with *him* when he told them so many personal things about us: how we'd met in rep at Eastbourne, had been married at St Stephen's Catholic Church, Taunton, as if these weren't innocuous facts, a matter of public record. Surely, he said, I could understand why my friend felt the need to lie so copiously?

Yes, I said sullenly. I could see why she wanted to lie to the newspapers, in *public*.

And now she was back, an audience for his ego.

"No, do tell," Suza said.

"Oh, not that tired old story!" I blurted out.

Don looked hurt. Usually I encourage him to tell his best theatrical anecdotes, especially if they involve actors people had actually heard of, since it gives them a vicarious brush with fame and they like that. "Suza hasn't heard it," he pointed out.

"Well, I have. Nine million times."

"Don't listen, then. You'd like to hear it, wouldn't you, Suza?"

She looked bemused. "I am perfectly willing to hear it."

"Good. That's settled, then." He sat back, moving into expansive mode, and began. "Mine was a small part."

"I've heard that, Andy!"

"Very funny. Anyway, my main bit was in the second act and, one midweek matinee, there was an old lady in the third row who was clearly totally deaf."

I got up, went to the sink and began to wash up the lunch things savagely. I made so much noise that I might have been totally deaf.

Don merely spoke more loudly. One thing he can do is project his voice. "Every time she made a remark to her companion it reverberated round the auditorium. Then, halfway through my big speech, she suddenly bellowed, 'Is that Lady Olivier in the big hat? She's changed a bit since *Gone With the Wind*, hasn't she?'"

Suza began to laugh. "What happened?"

"Well, the whole cast corpsed except for the incomparable Joan, who just kept on acting. She's a lovely woman and a real professional. I was playing her son and she asked me when I would be back and I was supposed to say, 'That, madam, is in the lap of the Gods,' before exiting with dignity. In the event I spluttered 'I dunno!' and ran off the stage."

Suza nodded approval, savouring this tarradiddle like a fine wine. "That's a good story, Andy."

"You know what? They didn't ask me back the next year!"

In a bored tone I said, "Coffee, anyone?"

It *is* a good story; trouble is it isn't a *true* story. Or at least it *is* true, but it didn't happen to Don; it happened to Toby Richards. Don has never met Joan Plowright. He has no idea if she is a lovely woman or a total bitch.

I made a pot of coffee. I looked at them both, sitting at opposite ends of the kitchen table, so pleased with themselves. Suza would probably borrow the story and put it in one of her books, thus making it doubly untrue.

How can I go on surrounded by people who *lie* for a living?

# I don't think that's funny

On Monday morning the weather was dry and bright and Don got up early, saying he was going to the golf club. After a quick breakfast, he slung his clubs in the car and called out, "Expect me when you see me. I'll get lunch at the nineteenth hole."

"What have you got in that carrier bag?" I asked.

"Oh, just my silk suit. I thought I'd drop it in at the dry cleaners to get it taken in a bit. It's too loose for me now, you know."

"But I can do that," I said.

"It was expensive, Jen, even in Hong Kong. I think it's best to leave it to the professionals. Don't you?"

I felt hurt that he didn't trust me to take in his trousers. "I see," I said stiffly. "Well, I expect you're right. Bring back a paper." I was still *persona non grata* at the post office, which was inconvenient. I felt cut off from village life. Don was tolerated. I expect Mrs Price felt sorry for him, married to a foul-mouthed harridan like me.

He waved acquiescence and drove off, leaving the gate open. I didn't bother to go out and shut it although for some illogical reason I felt safer with it closed, as if the portcullis was down and the drawbridge up at my castle.

I busied myself around the house but it was only half an hour later that I heard the sound of wheels on the gravel, a heavy vehicle. Suza's Land-rover, I thought with sinking heart. More make-believe.

But when I peered carefully out of the spare room window, wondering if I could pretend not to be at home, I saw the white open-backed van with moss-green lettering of Zebedee Landscapes. Aysgarth was driving. He came to a halt by the front door and got out. There was no sign of John the silent, perpetrator of crimes unknown but imaginable.

I went quickly down the stairs and opened the front door as the bell rang. Hugh stood with his back to me, surveying the work he, or rather John, had done. He wore jeans, a black T-shirt and a black leather jacket, his hands thrust deep in the pockets. I stared once more at the spectacle of his enormous feet as he turned round.

"Good morning," I said. I held out my hand.

"Hi." He didn't take my hand but held up his own saying, "I'm not armed!"

"Yes," I said, withdrawing my hand. "It is rather a silly custom." He had made me feel foolish and I resented that.

"I never feel my hands are clean enough for a lady."

Suza once told me that a lady is a woman who does as she's told.

"I came to see how the new lawn was settling down and how the flower beds are shaping up."

"Be my guest."

I followed him down the front garden. "Someone's walked across here," he said, crouching down. "I did ask you to be careful."

"I know. Sorry. I forgot." I'd stamped down the turf and raked over the beds and thought you'd need X-ray vision to notice the damage, but clearly Hugh Aysgarth was Supergardener.

He glanced up sharply. "How could you *forget*?"

I wanted to say, "Look, it's my garden and if I want to trample on it, I shall." Instead I said, "It was foggy."

This was hardly an adequate explanation, as if I might get lost between the gate and the front door of a house I'd lived in for fifteen years, but he said, "Oh, well. No great harm done. Have you decided on the roses?"

"I've made a list. You'd better come in."

He followed me into the kitchen, walking too close behind me, and I fetched the list I'd made of replacement rose bushes. He read it quickly, nodding approval. "I know a good supplier out Lowestoft way. I'll drive over and get them this afternoon then we can prepare them and plant them by the end of the week. November will soon be over. Time is pressing."

"Christmas will soon be upon us," I said, because it was the sort of thing people did say at this time of year. We both stood awkwardly for a moment. Clearly there was something else on his mind but I couldn't think what it might be. "I hear you were at school with Georgie Apter," I said finally, for something to say.

"Oh, yeah. For a while." He grinned boyishly, running his hands through his thick hair – no ponytail today. He added proudly, "I got expelled. Always a bit of a rebel, that's me."

*Oh, grow up*, I thought. I realised that if he'd been at school with Georgie he must be older than he looked.

I've noticed increasingly that people don't seem to want to reach adulthood these days, delaying marrying and having children and settling on a career until well into their thirties. I've heard people complain that their grown-up children won't leave home, hanging around playing gooseberry when they'd been looking forward to a quiet middle age, the two of them.

When Bill and Penny Gammon's two daughters married in a double wedding a few years ago, they promptly sold their five-bedroomed house and bought a two-bedroomed cottage. "They're welcome to visit," Penny had told me, "but not to come to stay."

Let alone to leave their husbands and return to the shelter of the parental roof.

Aysgarth finally came to the point, fishing in his pocket to produce a piece of paper. "I wondered if I might leave my bill for the work we've done so far, Mrs Donleavy?"

"Oh, of course." Strange that the rebel should be embarrassed to ask for money, like any middle-class man of his age.

I opened out the invoice. The amount at the bottom seemed huge but as it wasn't broken down – so many hours labour @ so much an hour – there was no real way of telling. I didn't know what price Don had agreed with him, but he was standing there expectantly so I said, "Let me get my chequebook."

"Cheers. Much appreciated."

After all, he'd have to fork out for the roses, which wouldn't be cheap, and there was still a lot of work to be done. If he was overcharging me now, the man of the house would sort it out later.

"Business good?" I asked as I made out the cheque.

"You know how it is. When times are hard, money spent on the garden's the first thing to go, deemed non-essential; but a couple of years' neglect can undo a lifetime of care . . . like with a marriage."

I didn't respond to this odd remark.

"Cash flow," he concluded, apologetically. "Always cash flow."

"Perhaps you vandalised my garden yourself," I said with a laugh, "provide yourself with a few days' work."

Blood spread through his pale cheeks like jam in rice pudding. "I say," he said, his public-school accent becoming more pronounced, "I don't think that's funny, actually." I stammered an apology. "There are dozens of gardening contractors in the *Yellow Pages*. I couldn't know your husband would choose me."

"Really." I went to lay a hand on his arm, then thought better of it. "It was a joke and a stupid and thoughtless one." I was glad when he left. I didn't detain him by offering him coffee. He made me uneasy.

"Who was that on the phone?" I asked Don that evening.

"Bloody Toby Richards," he said crossly.

"What? Calling from Lala Land?"

"No, that's the trouble. He was calling from the flat in Covent Garden to tell me that he was home for 'a month's furlough' and the flat wouldn't be available again until the New Year. Oh, and how about a piss-up while he's here? Seems you're not allowed to drink in LA these days, not politically correct, and every other person you meet is in a twelve-step programme."

"Well, you've no real reason to go to London before New Year," I pointed out. "There's no work lined up."

"Don't rub it in! Might have been nice to snatch a few days before Christmas, see some plays." He put his arms loosely round my waist. "Take my lovely wife out to dinner, to the opera and the art galleries."

"We could stay at a hotel."

"Oh." He let go of me and turned moodily away. "It can wait till next year."

He clearly thought that Toby was being selfish, coming home at short notice and wanting to use his own flat. When you're given something on a plate it's not long before you start taking it for granted. Even so, I thought he seemed unreasonably put out by it. Toby's extraordinary generosity in loaning him the flat for so long had fled straight out of his mind.

# A bit weird

Driving back from Woodbridge in the second week of December, I passed through the neighbouring village of Oldbourn and spotted the Crosses drawing up at their converted barn in Tim's BMW, two identical tow-headed boys in the back. They hadn't been in touch since the dinner party, except for a brief and stiff note of thanks from Claire, and they'd certainly not invited us back.

On impulse, I signalled and pulled my car into their driveway after them. It was time to build bridges, to offer olive branches. I got out of the car. They looked surprised as they recognised me and I greeted them heartily. "Don't expect to see you here on a weekday."

Tim nodded at his sons. "School broke up today. We drove down to fetch Peter and Simon. Thought we might as well snatch a few quiet days in the country before the horrors of Christmas."

"You're not spending Christmas here, then?"

"'Fraid not. Horrors of Claire's family home in Yorkshire and nine million of her rotten relatives."

All this was said without any lowering of the voice and I saw that Claire evidently agreed with every word of this abuse of her family.

The two boys sniggered and one of them – though there was no knowing if it was Simon or Peter – rolled his eyes and said, "Auntie Jackie!" in an emphatic tone, while the other stuck a finger into his mouth and mimed gagging.

I sympathised. I too had childhood aunts.

"Why don't you come in and have a cup of tea," Claire said. "It won't take us a moment to unload the car." I had no difficulty in working out that this invitation wasn't sincerely meant, but I accepted it anyway.

"Oh," Claire said. "Well . . . can you two boys manage the unloading by yourselves?"

Obviously they could since they opened the boot obediently and began to take out boxes of food, much of it ready-prepared – lasagne, casseroles, fish pies – from the supermarket. I saw that there were also a couple of trunks.

Claire unlocked the door, asked me to wait on the mat while she switched off the burglar alarm and led the way into the kitchen. She flung her bag down on the floor, filled the kettle and set it to boil. Tim joined us a moment later, leafing through a quantity of post that had arrived since their last visit.

I thought it must be downright tiresome to have two homes.

When the food was stowed away the two boys said politely that they were going upstairs to play with their computer games. Clearly manners were still taught at prep schools. Claire watched them go with the eye of ownership, then turned to me, as if she might otherwise burst and said, "We've just heard. They've both got scholarships to Winchester next autumn."

I was genuinely pleased for them although I wouldn't have dreamt of sending any child of mine away from home for weeks on end. Twins, of course, have each other, which must make life easier. I wondered where the boys got their brains from. Not from Tim, I thought, unless he was brighter than he seemed and lived on a higher plane of silver options and plastic cork futures.

I'd never seen the inside of the Cross house and now made the necessary overtures to being offered a guided tour, backing Claire into a corner where she frowned and said the place was surely an absolute tip as they hadn't been down for three weeks but I was welcome to look round if I must . . . if I liked, that is.

Tim, to my surprise, volunteered to act as guide. He led me into the high-vaulted room that rose the full height of the barn and served as the main sitting area. "Wonderful acoustics," he said. He carolled the first four notes of Beethoven's Fifth to prove it and they echoed into distant corners. "You want anyone, you hardly have to raise your voice."

I said, with all honesty, that it was beautiful and he looked pleased. "Designed it myself," he said. "Took years to get it the way we wanted it."

Open staircases led up on either side of the fireplace

to a gallery off which were a number of bedrooms, Tim's study, Claire's study and a playroom for the children. I examined each room with great care, although I didn't have the temerity to open cupboards. I was afraid those four Beethovenly notes might leap out at me.

His study seemed to be a genuine example of the paperless office, except for the fax machine which had overflowed onto the floor. I waited while he picked the papers up and placed them in a tidy pile on his desk without bothering even to glance at them. "Those can wait till after supper," he said with a rueful smile.

"You must work awfully hard."

"We're putting in more hours than we dreamt of in the giddy eighties," he said. "I seldom get back to the Barbican before eight p.m."

"That's what you get for voting for Thatcher," I said.

I saw the necessity for boarding schools. How could either he or Claire cope with two growing sons and such impossible hours? But then it hardly seemed worth having children if you weren't going to see them until they were grown up.

"If it's a volatile time," he concluded, "I wait for the Far Eastern markets to open, see which way they're trending." He looked far too young to be the father of those two huge sons and to wield so much of other people's money.

"Have you got a typewriter?" I blurted out.

"A typewriter!" he echoed. He couldn't have been more astonished if I'd asked if he kept a barouche landau and a pair of matched bays to pull it. Or would it be four bays? "'Fraid not," he said. "Everything done on computer here. Why? Did you . . . er . . . want to write a letter, or something?" He looked doubtful and said, "I can show you how to use the word processor," clearly not believing that I would be able to cope with anything so complicated.

"Oh, no!" I said, feeling foolish. "I just . . . wondered."

As he led me back downstairs, he said, "I read one of your friend Suza's books."

"Did you?" I was surprised.

"Of course I never read fiction as a general rule," he added hastily, in case I should get the wrong idea about him. "Haven't a lot of time for reading of any sort, come to that, and what's the point of something that's made up, that isn't true?"

What indeed?

"But I thought, as one had met her, I mean . . . Well, frankly, I thought it was a bit weird." I patted him comfortingly on the arm and he gave me an odd look. I realised he thought I was a bit weird too.

He ought to realise by now that Suffolk *is* weird.

We went back to the kitchen and I had my tea and said I must be going. I noticed that Claire drank hers without milk or sugar, just the squeeze of a tired-looking lemon.

"See you at Mr Herzog's party, I expect," I said, on the doorstep.

Tim said, "*Excuse* me?" as if he were an American, or thought I might be.

So they hadn't been invited, had clearly not served

their apprenticeship as local residents. He'd invited Suza, though. Perhaps it was that the Crosses were part-timers.

"Have a good Christmas," I called out as I got into the car and they echoed this sentiment and Tim called out that I must bring Don over to dinner sometime in the New Year and Claire glared at him.

They were both much too busy, I realised, to have any idea what was going on in Stratford St James, or to send letters about it if they had.

## We all have our faults

Christmas is less of a strain for me than it seems to be for most women, since we spend it alone at home, and have done for almost all our married life. The first year we tried to please both families, spending the day itself with my parents in Bishops Lydeard, in the rowdy presence of my sisters and their husbands and children, then shooting up to Gillingham to spend Boxing Day with Don's mother in her lonely, underheated house.

We agreed, never again, although I'd enjoyed the oneupmanship of displaying my new husband, who was so much more handsome and amusing than my staid brothers-in-law and proved to Rita and Madge once and for all that little Jennifer wasn't a silly kid any more.

After that we stayed at home, giving preference to neither family over the other. We would sleep late on Christmas Day, probably we would make love. Then we'd brunch in bed on smoked salmon and champagne, exchange our small gifts, and take the dogs for a long walk. Only one dog this year.

Christmas dinner would be in the evening and we would

eat and drink more than usual. Since there was nothing to interest us on television, those unfunny Christmas sitcom specials and blockbuster films, we would listen to music afterwards, and he would read to me. I'd always loved to hear him read in his husky vibrant voice and on this one day of the year he would indulge me.

He would sit on the floor at my feet, a glass of Scotch at his side to 'lubricate the tonsils', his head moving slightly from side to side across the text like a spectator at a miniature tennis match. He has to wear reading glasses now but takes them off if anyone but me is in the house. He makes sure he is word-perfect when he turns up on set but, if he needs to consult his script for any reason, he excuses himself and hides bespectacled in the lavatory.

Vain? Well, yes. We all have our faults.

One morning Suza deliberately drew his attention to something in the paper. Unable to get out of it, he had to hold the newsprint close to his nose. Suza made faces at him, out of his eyeline, and we both ended up giggling helplessly. He knew we were laughing at him but he couldn't prove it.

I made mince pies and a cake. We'd long since agreed that neither of us liked plum pudding enough for it to be worth the trouble. We would have something lighter: oranges in Cointreau with my bitter chocolate sorbet, perhaps, or home-made tiramisu. I leafed through my recipe files, planning the meal, perfectly happy.

Until.

"I expect you'll be inviting Suza to Christmas lunch."

I almost choked on my coffee. "I'm sure she's made other arrangements."

"No, I asked her. She'll be on her own."

"She won't mind that," I said. "She's a loner."

"No one is really a loner, Jenny, certainly not on Christmas Day."

"But we always spend it by ourselves, the two of us."

"We don't want to get into a rut."

Couldn't he face being alone with me?

"And what do you mean, lunch?" I went on. "We have our main meal in the evening."

"As I say, a change is as good as a rest. We could invite a few more people, someone to stay. What about Toby, adrift in London on his own for a month? Then we can have that piss-up I promised him."

"There's no room."

"Don't be silly. We've got a spare bed and no one ever sleeps in it. What's the use of a house where the rooms are closed up? I hate that."

"Suza won't like Toby."

"Why shouldn't she? Everybody likes Toby. There's no harm in him."

I knew I'd already lost, that he would do as he chose, but I continued to protest. "It's our special time."

"A bit of company will do us both the world of good," he said, and left the room, thus winning the argument, as he usually did, by walking away. A moment later he popped his head round the door again and said, "Give me a shout when I can come and stir the pudding mixture and make a wish."

I laughed like a sob. I looked out a pudding recipe and made a list of the ingredients I lacked and drove to the supermarket specially to get them. It was too late to make a pudding; it wouldn't have time to mature properly. Serve him right.

It's not true that everyone likes Toby: *I* don't like Toby. We stayed with him for a couple of weeks when we first went up to London from Eastbourne, while we looked around for a rented hovel of our own. We slept on a lumpy and narrow mattress on his sitting room floor, but I didn't mind the discomfort since it was the first time I'd been able to lie all night in Don's arms.

Toby tried to talk Don out of marrying me. He was too young to settle down. The seas were full of fish, bigger and better fish. That sort of thing. Don told me about it openly; he thought it was funny, but I didn't. "Toby doesn't understand," he said. "You should pity him."

It didn't stop him asking Toby to be his best man, or stop Toby from accepting. He made a hypocritical speech at the reception about what a marvellous institution marriage was and how lucky Don had been to find the right girl so early.

He's been married and divorced twice and has a kid by another woman, a boy he seldom sees. So much for his theory that early marriages are doomed to failure.

Shortly after his second wedding he told me that he and his new wife had an open marriage. "Yeah?" I said.

"Does *she* know that?" And he said in the cold, sneering way he has, "You think you're pretty smart, don't you, Jennifer?"

Perhaps he would refuse the invitation: he was much too grand for us now.

That evening I asked Don to read to me and, to my surprise, he said, "So long as it's not poetry."

I said happily, "You choose."

He browsed among the Evelyn Waugh and read from *Decline and Fall* for me. I sat back with my eyes closed, smiling from time to time.

Toby accepted our invitation at once, to my disappointment, and it was agreed he would drive himself up on Christmas Eve. He also told Don on the phone that he was going to sell the flat, buy a place out of town – "a sort of country estate, I suppose you'd call it."

"Bastard!" Don said when he'd rung off.

Merry Christmas.

## We wish you a merry Christmas

It was raining on the night of Mr Herzog's party but that didn't deter us. We'd decided to walk down since Don had announced his intention of drinking large quantities of champagne and I didn't see why I should be left out, my stomach pains now no more than an unwelcome memory, although I'd been told to continue with the pills for another couple of weeks.

We put mackintoshes over our finery: I was wearing my Annabel Wu again and he his cream silk suit, taken in to fit the new lean Don Donleavy. I couldn't see that the 'professionals' had done such a wonderful job in the end; I was sure one hem broke unevenly over his calfskin shoes. I'd been into Ipswich to get my ends trimmed and my low-lights touched up at a quarter the price I'd paid in Kensington and I thought we made a pretty damned handsome couple.

I took his arm and we walked together under his golfing umbrella. I was wearing sensible shoes but had a pair of giddy high heels in my bag to change into.

A couple of cars swept past us along the road, their

headlamps briefly gilding the rain. I didn't mind that none of them stopped to offer us a lift, although some were surely heading for the same place. Under the arc of the umbrella was a private place, a cosily self-contained world.

The Old Rectory was in Christmas mood: the wreath on the door, the huge tree in front of the French windows at the back with its tartan ribbons and its white candles, the mistletoe hanging in every doorway. Where had he found those sprigs of holly with so many berries? I'd searched the lanes for miles around but it was a lean year and I refused to buy it in the market – that was cheating.

The choir of King's College, Cambridge sang superb carols to us from a black CD player which was tucked tactfully away on a high shelf. The sound came at us from the four corners of the room, now whispering, now swelling; now sad, now joyful. There was birth and, prefigured in it, crucifixion and death.

Mr Herzog wore black evening trousers and a red velvet smoking jacket over a white silk shirt with ruffles; he looked dashing with his sweep of white hair resting on the collar. "I am *so* pleased," he said. "So pleased you could come." As if the favour was all on our side.

Are you queer, I wondered? Or did you never meet the right woman? How odd to go through life – through more than seventy years in his case – alone, not to be first with anybody. On the other hand it was far odder, perhaps, that anyone ever found someone they could bear to spend their lives with; and yet most people did.

If he was gay, would that make him more or less likely to be the sort of person who sent anonymous letters? Probably neither.

I knew that his name was David since the invitation said so – David Herzog At Home, since an English gentleman doesn't bestow the title of mister on himself – but I'd never heard anyone address him by it. He was on good terms with all and intimate terms with none.

We were gathered, as always, in the huge reception hall at the back of the house. What did he do with all this space, I asked myself? The early vicars of Stratford St James had clearly been philoprogenitive; but one old man, alone?

The velvet curtains were closed against the wet night. Later he would light the candles on the tree and give us clever little presents.

Mrs Price was there. A truce was called, nothing permanent, the two of us singing "Silent Night" at each other from opposing trenches. Machine-gun fire could be resumed tomorrow until eventually someone surrendered. Me, probably, since she had things I wanted such as newspapers and gossip; while I, on the other hand, had nothing that could possibly interest her.

Suza was there and looking handsome, leaning easily against the mantelpiece sipping champagne and talking to Colonel Apter. Leo's father clearly found her attractive, glowing in her conversation and fiddling with his military moustache. After a while he took her glass to refill it and I saw him squinting at the mistletoe over the fireplace with a hopeful eye.

I knew that Mrs Apter wouldn't be there since she seldom left the house, this self-imposed imprisonment being, as far as I could make out, more psychological than physical. I spotted Leo in the distance, though, with, to my surprise, Hugh Aysgarth.

I was mildly shocked. An invitation would have been sent to 'Colonel and Mrs Harold Apter and Miss Leonora Apter'. For Leo cavalierly to bring an uninvited guest with her to Mr Herzog's famous At Home struck me as little short of lèse-majesté. Would there be a suitable present for Hugh – a new pair of secateurs, perhaps?

Suza disappointed the Colonel by coming over to join us, offering her cheek to us both. "Jennifer! There you are at last. Hello, Andy."

"Hello."

Her spicy scent made me sneeze and I had to turn my head away.

"Excuse me!" Was I becoming allergic to her?

"What ferocious shoes!" she said. "How can you walk in them?" She opened her eyes wide; brown and gold eyeshadow flickered up to her brows and out towards her temples, enlarging them, enhancing their whisky colour. Her mouth this evening was big and red. She wore black harem pants with black suede pumps and a sleeveless top in some silvery material. Her arms were plump but firm.

If I were a butcher, I would pinch them and say, 'There's good eating there'. A number of silver bangles jangled round her wrist.

I assumed her question to be rhetorical so didn't bother to answer it. Balancing on ridiculous heels is the sort of useful tool you picked up at drama school. Like models, actors have to be able to smile grimly in the most uncomfortable costumes. Don once took over a minor film role at short notice when the original choice broke an ankle. He spent two weeks sweating under studio lights in a dress uniform that was a size too small and shoes that pinched his feet.

And did he complain? Well, yes, of course he did; but only to me.

"You've forgotten to shave your armpits," Don pointed out uncivilly.

"I didn't *forget*."

He sighed. "Sad feminist. How does uglifying herself make a woman's lot better?"

"Male chauvinist warthog."

"Now, now, children," I said. "If you can't play nicely together, I shall send you both home."

Mr Herzog joined our group at that moment and accepted our compliments with his usual grace. "Mrs Darc," he said, "you don't seem to have a glass of champagne. That is the most appalling and unforgiveable lapse!"

"Harry Apter went to fetch me a refill," she explained, looking round for her missing squire.

"No matter." Mr Herzog signalled to a hired waiter and procured her a fresh glass.

"I assumed you were Jewish," Suza said, "because

of your German name, but I've seldom seen Christmas celebrated with such verve."

I stared at her. I'd been longing to ask Mr Herzog about this for years but had never plucked up the courage since it seemed a bit personal to go around asking people about their beliefs.

Mr Herzog, however, was not in the least offended by the bluntness of the question. "My parents were committed Communists," he explained, "and gave up their religious practices before I was born, so I am Jewish by race only. I wasn't even circumcised, since my parents had come to think it a barbaric custom. Of course Mr Hitler wasn't interested in that. When the SS come knocking at the door, my dear Mrs Darc, it's no good saying, 'I don't celebrate Chanukkah. I am a Cavalier and not a Roundhead. Go away.' "

"So you were arrested?"

He shook his head. "I speak metaphorically, I'm glad to say. My parents and I left Munster in 1935, when I was thirteen, and settled in Manchester, no doubt as a homage to Engels, and I became an British subject in 1943."

He began to sing softly, his voice warm and rich, not cracked and thin as with so many old people. " 'In spite of all tempta-a-tion to belong to other na-a-tions; I remain an English man.' " He broke off. "And so on and so forth. Ahem. Excuse me. I cannot hope to compete with the exquisite youths of the choir."

He looked round his room with satisfaction. "I'm not,

of course, a Christian any more than I am a Jew and I abandoned the Marxist religion of my mother and father – much to their chagrin – to embrace capitalism wholeheartedly, first in an insurance office in Liverpool, then in the City of London. I am a heathen, Mrs Darc. *Der grosse Heide.* A glorious pagan."

"Me too," she said.

"And Christmas is essentially a pagan festival, the propitiation of the winter gods."

"The feast of the Invincible Sun," Suza said.

"Is that what they call it? I like the sound of that."

"Isn't it frightening," I said, to both or neither of them, "to believe in nothing?"

His wise old eyes were full of compassion. "Frightening? No. Not at all. You would call yourself a believer?"

"I believe in something," I agreed, "although I am not sure what."

"Yet you, I think, are afraid of many things, Mrs Donleavy."

"Yes," I said humbly, "I suppose so. But aren't you afraid of . . . of illness?"

"Cancer? Alzheimers? I hope I don't get these things but that's not the same as being *afraid* of them."

"Of being attacked in your own home by the sort of nihilistic young thugs that seem to roam the countryside these days?"

"The infamous motorbikers, you mean? Again, I take sensible precautions to deny them ingress, but to fear them would be to give them victory. Also, I gather from the local paper that arrests have been made in the matter of recent vandalism and charges brought. No doubt the feared hammer of Probation or Community Service will fall upon their heads."

"And Death?" I asked, exalting it with a capital D.

"Ah death: the best old friend, the right true end of life. No, Jennifer, I am not afraid of death."

I was so astounded at his calling me by my Christian name that I could think of no reply and he excused himself, saying he must mingle, and went to talk to Leo and Hugh Aysgarth.

"What a lovely old man," Suza said. "I think I shall marry him."

"Good idea," Don said sourly. "He must be worth a bob or two."

I mingled. I drank. I chatted, I flirted and I drank. Almost everyone I knew was there. By eleven the candles were lit on the tree, the other lights had been doused, and I stood leaning muzzily against the mantelpiece, alone at last, trying to focus on the groups of heaving humanity. My vision was blurred, as it had been occasionally lately, as Bill had warned me it might.

I suppose champagne didn't help.

Bill Gammon was now in colloquy with Colonel Apter. Penny had sequestered Hugh Aysgarth, no doubt to pick his brains about her rhododendrons. Leo was dancing drunkenly with Ruth Springer's husband to "Good King Wenceslas' – a hopeless task, I would have thought. Ruth herself was talking to our host. I thought that Aysgarth was wise to avoid dancing with *those* feet.

Which of you, I wondered? Which of you is my enemy?

I noticed the vicar and his 'wife', he self-consciously youthful in corduroys and some sort of fisherman's smock, she now more obviously pregnant in those same dungarees. They didn't seem worried by the fact that everybody else had dressed *up*. She stood leaning back slightly with her left hand on her bulge, while her other held a virtuous glass of mineral water. I knew that he already had three children from his first marriage. It seemed modern-day vicars could be philoprogenitive too.

Don and Suza were at the far end of the room. They'd been talking together for a long time. They were laughing a lot. They were standing closer together than usual, but then people did that at parties, if only to hear.

I saw Suza raise her arm to fiddle with her hair, saw the burst of dark fuzz in her armpit that Don had referred to. I didn't find it ugly. Don had taken his jacket off and I could see the faintest hint of sweat circles under the arms of his blue shirt. The room seemed warm.

The vicar came my way, the Reverend Robert Baker, looking for an ashtray for the dangerously long burn-down of his cigarette. He was about fifty, getting flabby, losing his hair from the top a tuft at a time and growing it further down his cheeks to compensate.

About Don's age, I thought dispassionately, but what a difference. What woman could desire those big hairy hands on her body, stroking her breasts and fingering her cunt while asking God to forgive him his lust? "Hello, Vicar," I said.

"Bob, please. Hello, Jennifer. How are you?"

"Oh, you know. Fine, really."

"We saw your husband in *Inspector Crane* on Sunday."

"Really?" I said. "Shouldn't you have been taking a service? Isn't that what they pay you for?"

"Oh, yes, but Nancy video-ed it for me. Can't miss *Inspector Crane* – high spot of the week."

"What a dull life you must lead."

These were things I usually thought rather than said aloud. Since he didn't seem to hear or take offence at them, perhaps I *was* only thinking them after all.

I am so tired of being well-behaved.

"I thought your husband was awfully good," he went on, "quite scary. Made me think I wouldn't want to meet him on a dark night."

"Quite right," I said, "and you don't want to fuck with me either."

He laughed too heartily at this and excused himself, pleading his wife's belly. His ash had fallen to the floor by now and I spread it about the polished boards with my foot, making a gritty grey layer. I closed my eyes to slits, the better to focus on the man you wouldn't want to meet on a dark night. I saw Suza remove something – a hair, a piece of lint, something invisible – from his collar. It seemed so deliberately intimate a gesture.

Suddenly the lights came on. Mr Herzog clapped his

hands to announce the time of the present giving, standing happy and proud under his Norwegian spruce. I saw Don and Suza look up, startled at the illumination. They saw me watching them. I saw the guilt in their faces. And then I knew. My anonymous correspondent had been right: how could I have been so blind?

Liars, I thought. Filthy liars, the pair of you, with your sick friends in Hammersmith and your phoned-out pizzas, your endless *golf.*

I looked round at the throng of people surging forward greedily for their gifts. How dare he, I thought? How dare he gather us together here and dole out presents as if we were his estate workers, his servants. Nasty, wrinkled, ugly old Jew.

You know, don't you? All of you. You've known for months. You've been laughing at me behind my back. Penny tried to drop a hint at the dinner party and later, that afternoon in the Butter Market, with her talk of poisoning. She's my friend. Even Bill remarked how he'd seen Don out walking Aggie late at night *down by Madder Cottage.*

How could I have been so blind?

I saw the vicar lighting yet another guilty cigarette, standing well away from his wife so as not to expose her and the baby to passive smoking. He avoided my eye and whispered something to his wife who stared across at me with her pale eyes. I saw Don looking covetously at him across the room, fidgeting for a fag.

That was why he'd given up, the real reason: because it affected *her* asthma.

"What were you and Suza plotting together for so long in your corner?" I asked him on the way home. Cunning, you see: making like I didn't suspect a thing, that they were getting away with it. They weren't the only ones who could be cunning.

"To take the Woodbridge bridge club by storm next year," he answered smoothly. He laughed. "You know, that's not easy to say when you've had a few. Woodbridge bridge bridge bridge club. Woodbridge bridge wood." He put on his Mickey Rooney voice. "Hey, Judy, let's put on a show in the barn!"

He was happy, I thought savagely, as we turned into the garden, past the stark outlines of the new rose bushes; he was bloody happy.

Liar.

The rain had drifted away in the strong north-easterly winds, leaving a clear cold night, and our way back was moonlit.

Sire, the night grows darker now, and the wind grows stronger. Fails my heart, I know not how, I can go no longer.

# Cuckold's point

I lay awake on my back, seething. He slept beside me, restless from so much champagne, but fast asleep nonetheless.

Aggie had demanded food on our return and, although I didn't usually feed her so late at night, I stopped in the kitchen to spoon a little extra into her bowl, to delay bedtime. So by the time I got up Don was already asleep, his clothes strewn anyhow on the floor, his breathing harsh in the quiet night of our remote home.

I went to the bathroom and washed and cleaned my teeth without haste. I got into bed beside him. I knew I wouldn't sleep. I lay twisting the ring on my finger in an unending circle, the exquisite diamond eternity ring he'd given me for our silver wedding in January, to eclipse the tiny solitaire engagement ring that had been all he'd been able to afford in 1970.

I could see it now, see how it had been: the first glances of recognition, the accidental touch of hands passing mugs of coffee, an exchange of electricity.

And I, myself, no doubt, bringing things to a head,

one evening when rain unexpectedly fell by bedtime and I said, "Don will run you home, won't you, darling? It'll only take him five minutes."

I could have taken her myself. Why did I think it was a man's job to be a taxi service on a dark country night?

*The brief journey back to Madder Cottage, neither speaking until, 'When and where can we meet?'*

*'Tell me where and when and I shall be there.'*

*My husband, running his hand over his mouth, too ashamed to look at her. 'Jenny mustn't know, ever. It can't be anywhere round here, or Woodbridge or Ipswich, anywhere where she goes and people know her and might recognise me.'*

*'Where then? The coast? Aldeburgh?'*

*He shakes his head. 'Leo Apter works in Aldeburgh.'*

*'Damn!'*

*'Do you know the coast around Orford Beach?'*

*'A little. I've driven out that way with . . .'*

For we had been everywhere together that summer, so throughly had I let her into my home and my life.

*'There's a parking place, a picnic area, above the nature reserve at Havergate Island—'*

*'Cuckold's Point.'*

*'What?' She's startled him.*

*'That's what it's called. Cuckold's Point.'*

*He makes a wry face. 'How apt.'*

*'Not really, Andy. If it was Jenny I was meeting it would be* apt, *since only a man can be cuckolded.'*

*'Pedant!' It annoys him that she's cleverer than he is: annoys him and excites him. "Heading south from Orford, you pass a farm. It's easy to miss, lots of trees—'*

*She says impatiently, 'I'll find it. When? How soon?'*

*'Noon? Tomorrow?'*

*'Where will you be, officially?'*

*'Playing golf at Waldringfield.'*

*She nods. 'Golf, good. Listen: you get there first. When you see me drive in, if it's not safe, if there's anyone else there, anyone who might conceivably recognise you, drive out as if you didn't know me.'*

*'With luck it'll be deserted at this time of year.'*

*She gets out of his car. 'Tomorrow, then.'*

*'Tomorrow.'*

*There's no one at the picnic area since summer is over and, anyway, the place is badly signposted and hard to find. For once in his life my husband is punctual and his blue Sierra is already there when her Land-rover pulls uneasily through the tree-lined track and stops beside him.*

*He gets out, locks up, and climbs in at her passenger door. They don't exchange greetings. Instead he says, 'I don't know where we're going to go.'*

*'I feel bad about this.'*

I like to think that she said that but how can I know? Suza is amoral: she's reaching out to satisfy an appetite; why should she refuse my husband any more than she'll refuse a slice of cake from me? And she's there, isn't she? She kept the appointment.

*He says, 'Perhaps we should forget about it.'*

*She ignores him, knowing that he doesn't mean it, putting the car into gear and backing away from the edge. 'I've rented a cabin, by the shore, a summerhouse.'*

*'Those places cost the earth!'*

*'Not when the season's over. Anyway . . .' She shrugs. 'I'm not poor.'*

*'The winter season. Is that how long I'm going to last? You'll be tired of me by spring?' He acts with casual voice but his face betrays him.*

*She laughs. 'Who knows?'*

*He tells her about the flat in London, Toby's flat. She nods approval. She always has reasons, excuses for being up in London, as does he.*

*I bet he told Toby about it. I bet Toby had a good laugh. Pleased to be proved right.*

*A pause. 'Did you bring some condoms?'*

*He's startled. 'Surely you know I'm sterile. Jenny seems to tell you everything.'*

*'Haven't you ever heard of safe sex?'*

*'That was after my time.'*

I'm talking as if this were the first time he has betrayed me, but how can I know? It may be the fiftieth time.

All right. Let's see.

*'Don't tell me you've been faithful to Jenny for – what is it? – twenty-seven years?'*

*My husband drums his fingers on the dashboard. 'No, there've been girls, women, while I was on tour, on location, but never more than a one-night stand – a four- or five-night stand at most. They wanted no more from me than I did from them.' He turns to face her. 'This is my first* affair.'

*She nods, she thinks the distinction a valid one.*

*'So, I didn't think to get any,' he concludes, sensing frustration, an abortive end to the assignation, perhaps even* – dare I hope? – *relieved at the let-out.*

*'It's all right,' she says, 'I bought some in Woodbridge this morning.'*

*He says sourly, 'You think of everything.'*

*Rudimentary but adequate, that is the summerhouse. No heating, since it's intended for the peak season only and the owner was amazed that anyone should want it in the autumn. Suza told him she was an author and needed somewhere remote and atmospheric to work over the cold weeks.*

*She pulls up outside and they turn to each other.*

*Their lips meet for the first time, enquiring, then demanding. They hurry inside.*

*Her throaty laugh. "Jenny says you like to be seduced!'*

*The lack of heating doesn't matter since they will soon warm each other. She's brought drink as well as condoms, a bottle of good Chablis, but they don't need it and head straight for the bedroom.*

*Where I cannot bear to follow them.*

*Do they talk about me, when they're done? Laugh at my lack of experience, with her asking clinically if I'm orgasmic and he saying, "Mostly, but not like you. You're so gloriously uninhibited.'*

*'The way I see it—' she props herself up on one arm, running her fingers through the wispy hair on his chest '—this is the most intimate thing two people can do together. If they feel inhibited then they shouldn't be doing it, or not with each other.'*

*'How wise you are,' he says, only half mocking.*

*'You're a better lover than I thought,' she says. 'I thought you would be selfish.'*

*'Is that what Jenny said? Only I sometimes think she goes out of her way to picture me to people as selfish, conceited and inconsiderate.'*

*'Not to mention manipulative.'*

*'No, don't let's mention that.'*

*'It wasn't anything she said, just . . . what I thought, from what I know of you.'*

*He turns to her again, rubbing himself against her*

*unsugared armpits. 'Why are we here,' he asks, 'in such an undignified posture, when you have such a low opinion of me?'*

*'Because I want you with my body and love you with my heart.'*

No, further I cannot venture.

*The train:*

*They settle back against the seats with a sigh. There's no one else in the carriage. 'Why on earth did you bring her to the station?'*

'She *brought* me. *My car packed up yesterday afternoon. I told her not to bother to come in but she took no notice.'*

*'The passive-aggressive are oddly powerful. I don't think she suspected anything, did she?'*

*'Oh no,' he says. 'You lie like a pro.'*

*She says, 'I* am *a pro.'*

*She tells him what I said to her that time, in confidence, about how sex was always pretty much the same, how it would probably be the same with any man, and they laugh at my naivety.*

*'I would guess she's not adventurous,' she says.*

*Not like her.*

Smartening me up – poor, dowdy middle-aged Jennifer – so they can live in hope of finding another man to take me off his hands eventually, spare him the guilt. Smartening *him* up, with his diets and his workouts at the gym, to make him more appealing to his younger mistress. I was prepared to love him as he was, pot belly and all.

Why wasn't that good enough for him?

*The weeks go by. Can he bring himself to tell her he loves her as he so seldom does me? I bet he doesn't find those words so hard to say to her. 'I love you. I want to be with you, but I can't leave Jennifer. She couldn't manage without me. I can't tell her. It would be kinder to kill her.'*

*And Suza, who is so much stronger than he, takes a deep breath and says, 'Then that is what we shall do.'*

First a campaign of terror, to render me weak and unhappy and unable to defend myself. Which of them was it? Both, I suppose. It must have been her who set the fire, since he was away in Yorkshire then. It was probably her who brutalised the garden while he slept tranquilly at my side. I expect the 'Bitch' was her own flourish.

It must have been her who administered the poison, a little at a time, whenever I came to her house for lunch. How typical of Don to sit back and let the woman do the work.

But my puppy? My poor, tiny, loving Scamper ripped apart by a fox's claws or a big sharp knife? That could have been him.

And it was he who loved to tell people I was ill, preparing the path for later.

*I begged her to get help but she wouldn't listen.*

How could I have been so blind? I wasn't. I have known, somewhere deep inside, from the beginning. A wife knows, although there are things known that aren't admitted to the conscious mind.

Why else would I have sent those letters?

I have to face up to my darkest fear. *She* told me that.

# Victorian values

In the morning he said he was going out to play golf. "You're playing an awful lot of 'golf' lately," I remarked. I bet they call it that, a joke between them: 'How about a round of golf?' Or a good 'workout' at the gym.

"I feel I'm making progress at last," my husband said. "And now John Creedy has taken early retirement he's there most days and he gives me a good game – that bit better than me so I've got something to strive for."

Remember: it's the detail that makes the tale ring true.

He ruffled my hair. "Most wives'd be glad to get their husbands out from under their feet in the mornings."

"Have a good time."

He put his arms round me, unexpectedly affectionate, and said, "I love you, Jenny."

I didn't answer but laid my head on his shoulder, trembling with the strength of my need for him. I inhaled, wondering if I'd ever smelt that spicy scent on him without realising it. There was none there now. But there would be when he got back.

"Later," he said, and left.

There were four dozen Christmas cards on the table, waiting to be written and addressed, stamped and posted. All identical, classic: Victorian Suffolk in the snow – ice skaters with furry muffs, carriages with snorting horses, chestnut braziers and muffin men; a plain greeting, nothing religious, chosen to offend nobody.

We don't have winters like that any more; instead of crisp snow there's limp fog and a lot of rain. Were they real, those Victorian Christmases? Or idealised fantasies like Victorian family values?

I turned my back on them in disgust.

I called to Aggie. How would she manage without me, poor old girl who has known no other mother? I was going out this morning and it seemed likely, one way or another, that I wasn't coming back. There was no one to whom I could entrust her welfare, no one I could trust at all. I must take the kinder course with her and put an end to future suffering. She came waddling to me, swinging her silly ears, wagging her trusting tail.

She followed me into the garden. I told her "Sit!" and she sat. She'd been well trained.

I fetched the shotgun from the study. It was loaded, contrary to what he'd told the policemen. Wasn't that careless? Was that what was lined up for me? *I'm sorry, officer. I thought I'd better check it out after your men reminded me of it, and it went off in my hand. What a ghastly tragedy.*

I put the muzzle inches from her head as she stood with

her tongue hanging out, panting. The trigger was stiffer than I'd imagined and took all my strength, a finger from each hand with the butt braced against my chest.

At that distance I didn't need to aim; it wiped her head clean off. The power of the shot took me by surprise. It seemed to echo to hell and back but I knew that no one was in earshot or, if they were, they would think nothing of a gunshot in the country at this time of year.

Aggie died instantly and without a sound. There was a lot of mess. I wrapped her body in one of the green binbags I keep for garden refuse, since she was too big for a supermarket carrier, and left her under the apple tree for later burial.

I put the gun back in the study and went upstairs. One down, two to go.

# Boning up

Her Land-rover wasn't there, parked on the green outside Madder Cottage, but then it wouldn't be since she was meeting *him*. I had a key and I made no attempt at subterfuge but walked straight up to her front door and let myself in. Any watcher would think nothing of it, Jennifer Donleavy paying a morning call on her best friend, although she might smile to herself, this watcher, and think, 'Are you blind? Wake up and smell the coffee.'

The heating was on and the house felt stuffy. How wasteful, I thought, when she would be out all morning, warm in his arms, to heat an empty house. I turned down the thermostat.

I pushed open the door into her study, a dark room, the curtains pulled only half back, leaving a mere six inches of light. Her desk was covered in papers, sorted into piles. I clicked on the spotlight to illuminate them and my eye fell on some letters, crammed back into their envelopes, a tempting inch jutting out.

I picked up the topmost two, unfolded them and read

them, since the gathering of information – of intelligence – is an important part of any war. The first was from an address in Hammersmith, signed by one Agnes who reported on the progress of her sick mother and thanked Suza for her recent help and support. The second signature was almost illegible but I think it said Louise. She – Louise, Lucy, Lulu – poured passions of rage onto the paper about her lover's refusal or inability to leave his wife.

I put the letters down. I was not taken in. She'd meant me to see these, to read them, to back up the stories she'd told me, but I hadn't fallen into her trap. I know how easy it is to write a letter to yourself and pretend it comes from someone else. She'd even manufactured two different handwritings, neither like her own, which was clever, as I'd had to use the typewriter, but I was cleverer. I was too wily for her.

I went upstairs. I wasn't looking for anything specific. Don wasn't a man to write love letters, to commit himself to anything that would stand up in a court of law. There might be photographs. She had a camcorder. There might be obscene videos, the camera set on a flat surface and left to run while they 'played golf'.

I hadn't been to the upper floor, hadn't been in her bedroom since I'd had the guided tour back in the summer, soon after she moved in, in the first tentative offerings of friendship. The house had been a mess then, with half the floorboards up and ragged holes in the plasterwork.

Her room was oddly tidy, in sharp contrast to the rest

of the house. Don hates untidiness, fussing things away like an old woman. How could he think of setting up home with such a slattern? The room was bare, little beyond a big bed with a pretty patchwork quilt, hazy blues and mauves, standing on a stripped wood floor with a colourful rug.

I pulled back the coverlet and shook loose her nightdress. It was long and white, made of a heavy cotton with embroidery round the neck. Must have been expensive. Did men find that sort of thing a turn on, this virginal look? I knew so little about men. Shouldn't it be black silk wisps and stockings with suspenders for your illicit lover?

There was a table beside the bed holding a lamp, three or four books, some tissues, a glass of water and a bottle of aspirin. Just like my own bedside table. I picked up the books, three new paperback novels, their spines not yet bent back, and a much-thumbed Classic Library copy of *Tess of the D'Urbervilles*.

I flipped it open. On the flyleaf was written "Susan Drake – Form 5a – Hawkins Essay Prize – 1968." Under it a school stamp with a Latin motto: *Aquila non capit muscas*. I wondered what it meant.

Susan Drake: it seemed a perfectly good name. I put the books back where I'd found them.

There were no wardrobes. She kept those in the small room next door which she called her dressing room. She told me once that she had grown up in a house full of hideous great carved wardrobes and that they frightened her when she was wakeful at night, but that was probably a lie too.

I stared thoughtfully out of the leaded window down into the back garden. The irrelevant thought came to me: you can see there's a stream there because of the way the trees grow in a straight line. I never noticed that before.

I was too absorbed to hear the Land-rover draw up outside, to hear her let herself in at the front door.

"Jenny!"

I spun round. "What are you doing here?"

"I think," she said gently, "that I'm the one who's entitled to ask that. Not that you aren't welcome in my house, naturally, but—"

"You startled me," I said. "I didn't hear you."

"Evidently."

I heard a sneering voice and it was my own; it was as cold as space. "What's the matter? Did he let you down? Stand you up?"

She looked puzzled. "Who do you mean? I popped into Ipswich to get a new inkjet cartridge for my printer."

Very clever.

She looked me up and down. "Are you going somewhere special? You're all dressed up." I had my new outfit on, the fiendishly simple black jersey dress and copper jacket that she had chosen for me. The copper earrings hung from my lobes like talismans. She peered at me more closely since the room was dark, the windows small. "Did you look in the mirror when you were putting that make-up on? It doesn't seem right somehow."

I'd painted my face with theatrical make-up, daubing copper eyeshadow somewhere in the region of my eyelids, shimmering lipstick on my mouth.

"And your hair," she said, laughing, "is wild and tangled."

"I like it like this."

She held out her hand, the laugh dying in her throat. "In the circumstances, perhaps you wouldn't mind returning my spare key."

"I want to know one thing," I said, moving forward, away from the window. "I want to know if you planned it before you even came here. Had you met him before? At a convention, maybe? Did you come here expressly to take my husband away from me?"

"Jenny!"

"What was the plan, Suza? What had you and he concocted between you? Did you mean to kill me or merely to drive me back into the madhouse?"

"I don't know what you're talking about."

"Don't you? The fire in my sitting room, my poor puppy who never did you any harm—"

"The fire was an accident. It's the sort of thing that can happen to anyone. And the fox killed your puppy. You know that. Harry Apter shot it. You cannot imagine I would hurt your puppy, that I could hurt any defenceless animal."

"Why not? You're allergic to them. You must hate them. They make you ill."

"I'm not the one who's ill—"

"Then the weedkiller on my lawn—"

"They've arrested the people who've been doing the vandalism, Jenny. We were talking about it at David's party. Remember? You weren't the only victim, even if you were the only one in this village."

I wouldn't listen to her honeyed words. "The poison you put in my food, your lousy food, when I came here—"

"No one has been *poisoning* you, Jenny!"

"No? The pains have stopped since I no longer come to your house for lunch. Well, isn't that a coincidence?"

"They've stopped because you've been taking the anti-ulcer pills that Bill gave you."

"You both tried hard to stop me going to the doctor, didn't you, getting a proper diagnosis? But it was okay in the end because my doctor was on holiday and I saw dozy old Bill Gammon and he played along with the ulcer scenario beautifully."

Suza stood with her hands on her hips. "Are you sure he wasn't in the conspiracy too? . . . I'm sorry, Jenny. I can't take any of this seriously."

"He comes here to see you, in secret, at night, when he's supposed to be walking Aggie."

"He has been dropping in occasionally," she admitted. "He's been worried about you, Jenny. We both have. We think you've been under a lot of strain lately."

She'd regained her poise; it only made me hate her more. So glib, so plausible. "Sit down, Jenny. *Calm* down.

Let's go downstairs and I'll make you a nice cup of tea and then I'll phone Andy—"

"Don't call him that!" I screamed. "No one bloody calls him that. No one's *ever* called him that. It's a secret name, isn't it? An intimate name? A *lover's* name?"

"Jenny, Jenny—" She reached out her arms to me as if she would swallow me up in them. I knew in that second that it was her or me. I launched myself at her. She was much bigger than me, of course, but I took her by surprise – poor weedy Jennifer who wasn't a good enough wife for the great Will Davenant, I mean Don Donleavy – and we tumbled together down the twisting stairs.

We landed winded at the bottom. She was limping when she picked herself up. I had a sharp pain in my left arm. She hobbled towards the kitchen, making for the phone. I followed her.

It hadn't occurred to me to bring the gun with me to Madder Cottage: that would have been too humane. I wrenched the telephone cable from the wall and she was left with nothing but blank silence in her ear.

I knew where everything was in this kitchen. I opened the cutlery drawer under the worktop and took out a knife, a Sabatier knife with a short sharp blade, like a butcher's knife, like old Mr Gammon's boning knife.

I turned it in my hand – is this a dagger which I see before me? – and she bolted, straight out of the kitchen door and down the garden towards the stream. There was no other way for her to run. I was blocking the way back into the hall and the safety of the front door and the village.

I don't know if the riding had toughened me up or if her asthma was weakening her but I caught her easily and we slithered together down the slope towards the Madder. She clutched at a willow branch but it gave way under our combined weight and in an instant we were in the stream.

It was freezing and we both gasped at the shock. She was trying to catch her breath, needing her inhaler, unable to call for help, even if there had been anyone to hear. Her mouth was open, snaffling at oxygen with a nasty, greedy noise.

I pushed her head underwater and saw her swallow it like a fish. I lifted the knife and plunged it once, twice, I don't know how many times, into her great pear-shaped breasts under her indigo sweatshirt.

Her head came up for a second and she screamed like a baby expelling the devil at the font. I shall always remember her face, her cunning face: cunning because she showed nothing but astonishment and disbelief and sorrow and terror right to the end.

When I was sure she was dead, I climbed out of the stream, slipping on the muddy banks. My Annabel Wu dress was ruined, covered with brown slime. I would never wear it again. I tore if off and stood there in my bra and tights, too frantic to shiver.

The stream ran fast after the recent rain and the pink water was already on its way to the village pond while fresh water ran clear and true over her corpse.

This would do her career no end of good.

I went back to the house, to the phone in the bedroom, since the one in the kitchen was out of order. I dialled three nines and asked for the police. I told them calmly that I'd killed someone in self-defence. My friend shouldn't lie for two weeks undiscovered like old Miss Aspinall. That wouldn't be right. They told me to stay where I was and not to touch anything until they got there.

It didn't occur to me to try and contact Don. I went back downstairs and put the knife down on the table in case it alarmed the policemen. They might be no more than young boys. They would probably be Chris and his friend. Chris could pop round later and put Don in the picture.

I wondered if they would ask for *my* autograph now that I'd done something heroic.

I sat down on a kitchen chair, my feet in a pool of damp, as muddy stream water dripped from my body, and I waited.

The threat to my comfortable existence had been averted. I could start to rebuild my life. I felt a sense of great peace now that my ordeal was over.

# Afterword

Don returned from the police station that evening to sit numb in his kitchen, an untouched glass of Scotch precisely centred on the table before him. He was afraid to venture into the other rooms and witness the dismantling of the stage set he'd spent so many years creating. "The curtain rises," he said out loud, "to show the sitting room of a country cottage, simply but tastefully furnished, the home of a couple long and happily married, middle-aged now but contented."

And he began to cry.

There was no question of Jenny's being allowed home. Not tonight, not before the trial, not after. It was for the best, the superintendent – a man younger than himself – had said kindly. For her own sake, because she was a danger to herself and others.

"I had no idea," he'd repeated stupidly. "No idea that things had got so bad. No idea."

They'd all been surprisingly kind: the uniformed man and woman they'd sent to break the news to him, the superintendent who was nominally in charge as it was a murder case, the doctor who'd declared her fit to be questioned. They'd let him see her for a few minutes before she was formally charged and she'd run to him and thrown her arms round his neck and her eyes were shining.

"It's all right," she breathed. "It's all right, Don. Everything will be all right now. We're safe."

"Yes, my darling. Yes."

She wore some sort of overall, white and shiny, and her hair was damp, straggling to her white, shiny shoulders. He'd taken his handkerchief from his pocket and wiped her docile face, mopping off the clown's make-up that she wore, dirtying the white linen beyond redemption.

The evening papers had already got hold of the story.

**Mystery Death of Novelist**

**The death has been reported this evening of best-selling novelist Suza Darc. Darc, 45, a resident of the small Suffolk village of Stratford St James, was apparently found dead in a stream at the bottom of her garden this afternoon.**

**It's understood that a local woman, aged 48, who was found half naked at the scene, was taken to Woodbridge police station to help police with their enquiries and was later arrested. A police spokesman said that no further details could be released until a post-mortem had been held to determine the cause of death.**

As soon as he'd taken in what the young constables were

saying to him, been convinced that it was so, he'd called John Creedy, the man he'd being playing golf with. John was retired now but had been exactly the sort of small-town family solicitor that he needed at that moment. He'd asked half a dozen quick, calm questions over the phone, listened intently to the answers, and said he'd meet Don at the police station. By the time he got there he'd dug out his office suit and regimental tie and gave off an air of unruffled authority.

"Is there a history of mental illness?" he asked after he'd seen Jenny, listened to the bedraggled tale she'd told to the policemen in the interview room, to the smoothly whirring tape-recorder.

Don had explained about the two months in the psychiatric hospital after it had become clear that Jenny would be unable to give him children as she longed to do. She'd emerged from the place a new woman, reconciled if indefinably older, ready, at least on the surface, to accept his assurance that what mattered to him and had always mattered to him was to have her, and only her.

"But that was almost twenty years ago," he concluded. And he had tried so hard to protect and shelter her all this time.

John shrugged. "These things never quite go away, in my experience. Once there's been one nervous breakdown there will tend to be others." A path that, once trodden, is familiar and known the second time, easy to follow. "Better manslaughter on the grounds of diminished responsibility than cold-blooded murder," he added.

John had driven him home and volunteered his company for as long as Don wanted it but Don didn't want it. He'd offered to ring anybody Don asked for – a relation, his doctor, a close friend – but Don had no relations but Jenny and he needed to get used to being alone now.

He was going to be alone for a long time.

She was charged that night and the papers had the full story the following morning. The village had been saturated with reporters since the discovery of the body; since the arrival of the two constables answering what they thought must be a hoax emergency call, a babbling joke; since these two, ashen-faced, had led Jenny from the cottage to the waiting panda car wrapped in a blanket. They were camped on the green outside Madder Cottage. Mrs Price thought she'd died and gone to heaven.

**Neighbour Charged in Novelist Murder**

**Jennifer Donleavy, 48, has been charged with the murder of novelist Suza Darc in Suffolk on December 17th. Locals say that the two women had become close friends since Ms Darc's arrival in the quiet rural village of Stratford St James earlier this year.**

**'Thick as thieves, they were,' was the verdict of the local postmistress, Mrs Pauline Price, 'but it doesn't surprise me that it should come to this falling-out when Mrs Donleavy's been behaving so oddly lately. And her practically naked**

**too. I knew there had to be more to it than met the eye.'**

**Donleavy is the wife of actor Andrew Donleavy, best known for his depiction of Captain Will Davenant in cult TV series *Space Pirates.* Mr Donleavy was not available for comment.**

Jenny half naked, how they loved that. How the story would grow and soar from that fact and become something quite other than the unhappy truth, something sordid and prurient.

The dog's body was inexplicable, among so many inexplicable things. When he'd mentioned it to Jenny she'd seemed not to know what he was talking about, perhaps unaware that there had ever been a dog. He'd dug a deep hole under the apple tree in the middle of the night and placed the remains of Aggie next to the rest of the graves. She'd needed a big hole and there'd been something restful about the rhythmic clunking of the spade into the winter earth, the protests of his under-used muscles.

It had exhausted him and he had slept for an hour or two before dawn.

He'd put off ringing her sisters, two women he particularly disliked. Neither he nor Jenny had seen them since their mother's funeral, conducting their family warmth via cards in December. They would be alarmed more than anything, if he was any judge, concerned that people would remember that this murderer was their sister, wishing they hadn't occasionally boasted that Andrew Donleavy was their brother-in-law.

They would be ashamed.

If he'd been told that some woman of his acquaintance had taken the life of a fellow human being, even by accident, he would have recoiled from her, from this most final of deeds, but it didn't occur to him to feel revulsion for Jenny or even for what she'd done. He didn't blame her for Suza's death: on the contrary, he blamed Suza for her breakdown and this disaster.

Couldn't she have understood that some people were fragile and that their lives shouldn't be meddled with? She, who claimed to be so wise.

He would be there. He would wait for her, because he loved her and he needed her.

"What will she get?" He'd rung John that morning after reading the report in *The Times* and blurted out the question without preamble, even to identify himself.

"Don, how are you? Did you sleep?" John had not passed beyond the social graces, trying to give his friend a foothold in sanity.

"I don't know. A little. Please. What will she get?"

John paused for a long time before replying. "Anything from a non-custodial sentence to life," he said finally. "Depending on what they charge her with—"

"But she's been charged with murder."

"For the time being. The Crown Prosecution Service will decide if there's a realistic chance of a conviction on that charge. Even if they go ahead with a trial for murder – and that would surprise me given her evident state of mind – the jury would probably convict only on a lesser charge, although one never knows. Sometimes you get a jury that's vindictive, or just plain stupid. If she's convicted of manslaughter than the judge has any amount of discretion as to her fate."

"A non-custodial sentence," Don repeated with hope rising in his heart.

"That's . . . unlikely, Don. In any event she'll need help. Treatment. Some sort of nursing home, for months, even years."

Don said, "Yes." He hung up.

He didn't want to read the papers, watch the news on TV, hear it on the radio, but he couldn't help himself. *The Times* carried a short obituary a few days later, delayed no doubt by a desperate scrabbling around for substantiated facts about this most mysterious of women. They used the same photo that had graced the recent interview with her and her smile struck him as knowing.

**Suza Darc was born Susan Ellen Drake in Greenford, West London in January 1952, the only child of a pharmacist. Although she was reticent about her early life, it seems that she attended a prestigious girls' grammar school but didn't go on to university, taking a job in a bank as a trainee cashier.**

**She appeared on the literary scene some ten years ago but only began to make a name for herself with the publication of her third novel, *The Four Friends*, five years later. Her**

**agent, Diane Gill, of Webster, Crane, Gill, said, "Suza liked to act eccentric, as if she thought that was the persona a writer should have, but she was a very ordinary, good-hearted woman, devoted to her friends. She would do anything for them. She had a unique talent, an individual voice, and her death has been a dreadful shock to everybody in the office."**

**Suza Darc died in mysterious circumstances in the garden of her Suffolk cottage a week ago. A local woman has been charged with her murder. She never married and is not thought to have any surviving family.**

"A bank cashier," Don said softly, "in Greenford. You should have stayed there, Susan Drake. You should never have set foot in Suffolk, never barged into our lives."

A good-hearted woman who was devoted to her friends and would do anything for them. And it had cost her her life.

He separated the newspaper into individual sheets and crumpled them. He placed them on the bonfire at the bottom of the garden and put a match to them. He stood and watched as the wind whipped pieces of what looked like hot black silk into the air, dancing around the hedges, settling on the walls that enclosed the White Cottage and protected it from the outside world.